Kotter's Back

E-MAILS FROM A FADED CELEBRITY TO A BEWILDERED WORLD

Gabe Kaplan

SSE

SIMON SPOTLIGHT ENTERTAINMENT
NEW YORK   LONDON   TORONTO   SYDNEY

SIMON SPOTLIGHT ENTERTAINMENT
An imprint of Simon & Schuster
1230 Avenue of the Americas, New York, New York 10020
Designed by Jane Archer
Manufactured in the United States of America
First Edition 10 9 8 7 6 5 4 3 2 1
Library of Congress Cataloging-in-Publication Data
Kaplan, Gabriel.
Kotter's back : e-mails from a faded celebrity to a bewildered world /
by Gabe Kaplan.—1st ed.
p. cm.
Includes bibliographical references and index.
ISBN-13: 978-1-4169-3502-5
ISBN-10: 1-4169-3502-9
1. Letters—Humor. 2. Electronic mail messages—Humor. 3. American
wit and humor. I. Title.
PN6231.L44K37 2007
816'.54—dc22
2007015466

FOR PATSY, WHO WOULD HAVE SAID, "WHAT ARE YA DOIN' WITH YOURSELF? WHY WOULD YOU SEND RIDICULOUS COMPUTER MAIL TO PEOPLE? IT'S DISRESPECTFUL AND DOESN'T ENRICH ANYONE. LIFE IS MORE THAN SILLY NONSENSE. SOMEDAY YOU'LL REALIZE THIS."

CONTENTS

INTRODUCTION

I came up with the idea for this book after receiving an unusual network television offer. Prior to this overture, the last network TV show I had worked on was an episode of *Murder, She Wrote* in 1984. (I was fine in my role as a comedian who is unmasked as the killer, but tensions arose when Angela Lansbury bitch-slapped me during lunch as I cut in front of her at the craft service table. Hey, I was hungry, and she wasn't keeping up with the line.) Since then, show business and I seemed to have had a mutual understanding—it didn't bother me and I didn't bother it. This policy worked well for twenty years, and neither side showed any interest in changing the agreement.

And then, suddenly, in 2001 I started getting multiple offers to be on television again. Why the renewed interest? Well, reality shows were exploding, and a very bright producer thought it would be a good idea to do a celebrity week. When it got solid ratings, they decided to go one step further and do a nostalgia celebrity week. If people got a laugh watching their favorite celebrities eat goat testicles, wouldn't it be even funnier if *old* celebrities were made to take a bite? I was asked to do most of these shows, but since goat testicles had been a staple of my diet for years, I didn't think it would be fair to have such a big advantage.

Then I got an e-mail from a talent coordinator, asking if I would like to participate in FOX's next episode of *Celebrity*

Boxing. The show was offering me $35,000 to get into the ring and try to pummel another overweight, sixtyish, D-list celebrity. The network had already aired two highly rated episodes—one featuring a fight between Ron Palillo and Dustin Diamond (Horshak vs Screech). They called it "The Battle of the Nerds," and a victory in that fight rocketed Diamond into careers in Internet begging and porn acting.

FOX saw its next "Pride and Glory" match as "The Battle of the TV Teachers," Howard Hesseman vs Gabe Kaplan. I believe Caligula would have deemed this match too distasteful for the Colosseum. FOX had ordered a third episode, and they were having trouble getting anybody interested in CB III (I can't imagine why). It seemed all the people crazy enough to do the show had already been on the first two episodes.

I sat at my computer to decline the offer, then suddenly said, "Screw it! I'm going to have fun with this." I mean, what was the downside—hurting my career? So I began my e-mail by saying how thrilled I was to be asked, that I boxed all the time but had become a Hasidic Jew and would have to fight wearing a skullcap and tzitzit. (A tzitzit is a body prayer shawl worn under a shirt so that only the fringes are visible.) I wrote that I didn't want to fight Hesseman, who was only about sixty, but would be happy to fight seventy-year-old Adam (Batman) West, or the eighty-year-old former *Diff'rent Strokes* star Conrad Bain. Plus, I explained, I could save the network money on expenses, as I generally traveled with my own trainer and cut man. I also asked to stage a press conference before the fight so my opponent and I could hype the match with a big show of macho posturing. We would trash talk about who was the better boxer/actor/comedian and be physically separated after having inflicted minor wounds.

When I was done compiling my list of demands, I hit send and my e-mail went winging off into cyberspace. I was quite surprised when he actually sent back an answer, addressing each demand point by point. He said yes to the skullcap and to my own corner men, and no to the tzitzit, the press conference, and West and Bain. (I guess sixty-five was the age limit for a celebrity boxing license.) I had to keep rereading his e-mail before I was convinced that he was serious! I fired back, stating that Hesseman would be okay, no staged press conference was okay, but the tzitzit was a deal breaker. They replied that I could enter the ring bare-chested, wearing it throughout my Michael Buffer introduction, but I would have to remove it just before the fight. He closed by saying they were eagerly awaiting my response. What could I do? I was hooked, powerless to stop this; it was just too much fun.

So, with one half of the fight card locked up, FOX tried to secure Howard, who told them to get lost. In fact, nobody FOX contacted wanted to fight. They tried actors who hadn't been on TV since *Love, American Style* went off the air, no dice. The situation got so desperate, an offer was actually made to Adam West. Hey, maybe he was crazy enough to do it; why should they care if the fight put the Caped Crusader on life support— these are ratings we're talking about! West said he was too old to box, but he would like to attend the match and provide commentary on the nobility of older men fighting. <<Pow!>> <<Smack!>> <<Sag!>> <<Cough!>>

In our next round of e-mails I suggested that I fight Dustin Hoffman in an effort to avenge Ron Palillo. My guy carefully and slowly explained to me the difference between Dustin Hoffman and Dustin Diamond, and said there was no chance of

Hoffman doing it. ("Yeah, definitely can't box . . . I'm an excellent basketball fan . . . definitely can't box . . .) He also added, "Fighting Diamond wouldn't be age appropriate." So I said, "Okay, I'll fight anybody my age except Jimmy Caan and Angela Lansbury. They're both too tough." I also warned them that if they didn't find the right opponent fast, I was going to say yes to *Celebrity Lancers*, the new celebrity jousting show. He poured on the flattery, calling me a legend, an icon, and a comedy giant. He assured me that my fan base would tune in by the millions to see me on *Celebrity Boxing* for some good clean fun.

I decided I had wasted enough of this guy's time. He really didn't seem like a bad person and, besides, he had a tough job. In my final e-mail I wrote that my doctor had advised me not to fight. He was disappointed but took it quite well.

My correspondence was for my own amusement and was never meant to be published. I wrote things and made requests that I thought were funny. (If my father were alive, I'd be in big trouble over the tzitzit.) But after rereading our surreal exchange I started to entertain the thought of doing a whole book involving funny e-mail correspondence. I got excited about the concept and sent out a few more test e-mails. When the answers that came back were just as funny as the *Celebrity Boxing* exchange, I dove headfirst into the project and worked on it for a little more than a year.

There had been similar books in the past that featured funny correspondence between an anonymous fictional character and his unwitting marks. But mine would be the first book to feature e-mails from a real person, one with whom most people had some degree of familiarity.

Checking my inbox every morning became an adventure. I never knew how people would react to what I had sent them. Most people seemed to take whatever I wrote at face value.

When I finished, I couldn't decide whether or not I wanted to publish the results. Some were just too over the top. I finally eliminated about half the correspondence and decided to go ahead with the rest. And that's what I have included in this book (though in some instances I have changed names or e-mail addresses). If you like the end result, e-mail me. If I e-mail back, don't take me too seriously. Remember, I could be writing another book.

Date:	Mon, 25 Nov 2002 17:10:24 -0800 (PST)
From:	"Gabe Kaplan" <gabe@gabekaplan.com>
Subject:	60th Birthday Parade
To:	pauleckert@siouxcity.com

Dear Paul,

During the four years "Welcome Back, Kotter" was on network television you'll be happy to know that your city, of all the cities in the U.S., gave it its highest average rating. It really is amazing when you think about it; the first year we were on opposite "The Walton's" and the rest of Iowa was watching that show by a fair margin. But not Sioux City! From the get-go you guys were firmly in the Kotter camp. I don't really know why it scored so high in your fair municipality, but according to Mr. Nielsen those are the facts.

Next March 31st, I will be celebrating my 60th birthday. Never thought I'd make it. To drum up some interest and excitement around this event, I thought a parade through your town honoring me would make a lot of sense. It hasn't been that long ago and a lot of people must remember. This would be something the whole city could get behind. The older folks could explain to the youngsters exactly who I am and why I'm part of the Sioux City heritage. Although I would like to help in the planning, it probably would be better for me to show up on the day of the parade to be surprised and delighted by your ingenuity and creativity.

I hope you'll say yes. I can't think of having my 60th birthday parade in any other place.

Seventy-six trombones led the big parade!

Gabe Kaplan
gabe@gabekaplan.com

Date:	Mon, 09 Dec 2002 17:34:49 -0600
From:	"Paul Eckert" <pauleckert@siouxcity.com>
Subject:	Re: 60th Birthday Parade
To:	gabe@gabekaplan.com

Hi Gabe,
To say the least, it was a surprise to hear from you Mr. Kotter! Being 40, I know your work and enjoyed it very much.

Sorry about the confusion with the blank e-mail and then the delay in response. Believe it or not, yes we are very interested in your visit and special event. Sioux City goes crazy over events like your suggesting. However, March 31 is often cold and snowy. Dave Bernstein, one of our community leaders, special event organizers, steel plant owner and all around great guy has suggested you lead our Big Parade in July. However, we are open to anything at this point.

We are interested in your response. Let us know what you think.

Paul
City Manager
Sioux City

Date: Fri, 13 Dec 2002 10:30:03 -0800 (PST)
From: "Gabe Kaplan" <gabe@gabekaplan.com>
Subject: Re: 60th Birthday Parade
To: pauleckert@siouxcity.com

Hi Paul,

It's probably hard for you to believe that you're 40 already. I bet you never thought you'd get that old. Wait until you're almost 60 and you're thinking about *your* 60th birthday parade. Forty will seem like Junior High.

There might be a slight confusion when I say next March 31st. I'm not talking about the up-coming March 31st; I'm referring to March 31st, 2004. It's just the way we express ourselves in New York.

I know you couldn't possibly have things ready for this upcoming March 31st. besides; nobody would describe a 59th birthday parade as a "special event".

Thank you for the offer to lead your Big Parade in July, but my slate is kind of full that month. I'll be competing in a senior triathlon in West Palm Beach and then I'll join my group's annual pilgrimage to photograph big horned sheep throughout the southwest.

If it were possible to lock in next March 31st (2004) it would give 15 months to plan a special event. All of the other Kotter cast members have already committed to being there. This could get national publicity. My 60th birthday parade should be in Sioux City. If we get unlucky with the weather, so be it. There's something about the Iowa way to greet you, and a little snow won't change that.

If you were to get 76 trombones and 110 coronets from the local high schools, I'll spend the next 15 months practicing to be "The one and only bass." That would get additional publicity leading up to the event, and when I modestly take my place everybody will be filled with great anticipation.

I said I'd let you plan the event, and I'm still willing to do that. I'm just throwing out these ideas to see what you think. If you want me involved with the planning, great! If not, no problem.

Of course I will handle all of my expenses. To get the other Kotter actors, we'd have to pay transportation, hotel and a daily food per diem. But if Sioux City finds this excessive, I wouldn't mind carrying some of the load.

Let me know what you and Dave Bernstein think. Incidentally, he's not the Dave Bernstein that first brought the Beatles to New York is he? He'd have to be my age, if he was.

Pleased you're interested. With a capital "P", and that stands for "Parade".

Gabe Kaplan
gabe@gabekaplan.com

Date:	Mon, 16 Dec 2002 17:54:19 -0600
From:	"Paul Eckert" <pauleckert@siouxcity.com>
Subject:	Re: 60th Birthday Parade
To:	gabe@gabekaplan.com

Hi Gabe,
Thanks for the note. We have got several promoters/organizers very excited about the parade/festival. Can I get your phone number and a few times that Dave Bernstein and I can use to make contact with you to discuss all of this in greater detail. We are getting fired up here in Sioux City!!!

Thanks,
Paul

Date:	Wed, 18 Dec 2002 14:06:19 -0800 (PST)
From:	"Gabe Kaplan" <gabe@gabekaplan.com>
Subject:	60th Birthday Parade Galapagos Break
To:	pauleckert@siouxcity.com

Paul,

It's great that you guys are excited about the parade. I'm anxious to hear if you like my ideas, or if these promoters you mentioned have their own thoughts. One thing I don't want to do is pose for pictures with kitchen appliances, or at an automobile dealership. That kind of stuff can stop any parade in its tracks.

Tomorrow I'm off for a celebrity golf tournament in the Galapagos Islands. I've never been there, so I'm really looking forward to the experience. Lets talk after the holidays and see if we can put this exciting event together.

Enjoy the seasons festivities and have a happy new year.

Gabe

Date:	Mon, 07 Apr 2003 15:15:56 -0500
From:	"Paul Eckert" <pauleckert@siouxcity.com>
Subject:	Re: 60th Birthday Parade Galapagos Break
To:	gabe@gabekaplan.com

Hi Gabe,
Haven't heard from you in a while. How are you
and how was your vacation? Things have changed
in the world since we last...

We are still interested in the 60th Birthday
Bash if you are. Let us know and we can get
together somehow. Our organizer Dave Bernstein
gets to California frequently so maybe we can
arrange a meeting sometime.

Thanks,
Paul

Paul,

Well, I'm past 59 and 60 is coming up around the bend. Let me tell you, man, it's scary! Thanks for inquiring about the vacation. I placed third in the golf tournament in the Galapagos and that's only because a lava lizard ran away with my ball on the 17th green. I got a great picture of it though!

I'm still very interested in the parade; I would love to meet Sid Bernstein if he comes to L.A. I feel we should get into the detailed planning stages by September. Remember, no posing with kitchen appliances or at car dealerships.

Let me know if you have any new thoughts.

Best Regards,

Gabe

Date:	Wed, 13 Aug 2003 11:12:50 -0500
From:	"Paul Eckert" <pauleckert@siouxcity.com>
Subject:	Sioux City Party
To:	gabe@gabekaplan.com

Hi Gabe,
Greetings from Sioux City! We haven't heard from you for a while. I hope you're doing well.

We are still very interested in doing a birthday bash! There are plenty of fun opportunities including that parade, using our new Event Center scheduled to open this coming December, our fantastic Performing Arts Theater. Sheryl Crow has come to it twice in the last year. Dave Bernstein was instrumental in it's recent rehabilitation.

You may remember that I mentioned my friend Dave Bernstein. He's a hell of a good community oriented guy and knows how to organize top notch quality events (with no appliance endorsements). We would love the opportunity to talk with you on the phone. Can you provide a phone number we can reach you at. Dave occasional gets to LA so that's a possibility also...

Can you call or provide a number we can reach you. Sioux City would love the chance to get you here. We think you would enjoy the event and the community's outpouring of support for you.

Paul Eckert
Sioux City City Manager

Date: Tue, 19 Aug 2003 00:43:52 -0700 (PDT)
From: "Gabe Kaplan" <gabe@gabekaplan.com>
Subject: Re: Sioux City Party
To: pauleckert@siouxcity.com

Paul:

Sorry for the confusion. You never answered my last email of April 7 so I thought you guys had given up on the idea. I chalked it up to a kitchen appliance having to be involved somewhere along the parade route.

I'm finishing up an interesting summer theatrical project. We've recreated the '50s television show "The Real McCoys" and I've been playing Pepino to rave notices. Wilford Brimley is playing Grandpa. He's a great actor, but he's always complaining about his ailments. I asked him if he'd attend the parade but he was noncommittal. He mumbled something about heart disease and oatmeal.

I'll be back home after Labor Day and we can talk then. Is Carl Bernstein going to be in L.A. in September or October? I'm so happy you wrote to me and that the parade is still on. I thought we were standing there touching noses and not seeing eye to eye.

Gabe
gabe@gabekaplan.com

Date:	Mon, 25 Aug 2003 07:52:25 -0500
From:	"Paul Eckert" <pauleckert@siouxcity.com>
Subject:	Re: Sioux City Party
To:	gabe@gabekaplan.com

Hi Gabe,
Thanks! We would enjoy the chance to talk with
you. If you have a few preferable time slots
just let me know and we'll work around your
schedule.

Thanks,
Paul

Date:	Mon, 25 Aug 2003 2:27 (PST)
From:	"Gabe Kaplan" <gabe@gabekaplan.com>
Subject:	Re: Sioux City Party
To:	pauleckert@siouxcity.com

Paul:

I'm headed back to Los Angeles next week. "McCoys" closes its run on Sunday.

I haven't heard back from you. Did you want to set up a time to talk?

It will be nice to finally hear your voice after all the emails.

Gabe
gabe@gabekaplan.com

Date:	Mon, 15 Sep 2003 18:00:26 -0500
From:	"Paul Eckert" <pauleckert@siouxcity.com>
Subject:	Re: Sioux City Party
To:	gabe@gabekaplan.com

Hi Gabe,

Sounds like you have been very busy and having fun!

I am certain you would have a blast here in Siox City. Folk in Sioux City all turn out for celebrations. I think it has something to do with being a bit isolated from larger metropalitan areas. You appreciate things more because there are less oportunities... Remember, everyone watched your show!

I will clear my schedule for anytime you would like to talk. My phone number here is 712.xxx-xxxx. Just let me know when you would like to talk. Our offer still stands, Dave and I would be happy to meet you in CA or Las vegas if that helps also.

Take Care,
Paul

Date:	Thu, 29 Jan 2004 21:14:43 -0600
From:	"Paul Eckert" <pauleckert@siouxcity.com>
Subject:	Re: Sioux City Party
To:	gabe@gabekaplan.com

Hi Gabe!
Greetings from Sioux City! It's cold here right
now (-5). I hope you're somewhere much warmer!

I hope things are going well for you! Speaking
on behalf of the Mayor and my friend Dave
Bernstein who I've mentioned before, we would
really, really, like to get you out here
to Sioux City. Dave is one our City's best
ambassadors and he'll be out in your area, along
with our Event Center Director Denny Gann, next
week. They would very much like to hook up
with to discuss some kind of wild Gabe Kaplan
celebration for your special upcoming birthday.

If we can't do your Birthday, we can have the
Country's first Gabe Kaplan "ALL City Fan Fest."
You have no idea how many folks would turn
out for something like that here in Sioux
City. If we do it right it would get national
attention.

We would like to hear from you ASAP to make
arrangements for a visit. If you any questions
about our city I encourage you to check out:
http://www.siouxcitytourismconvention.com/

As always, I look forward to hearing from you
and hope we can pull something off soon!

Paul
City Manager of Your Biggest Fan Base

BIG HORNS WANTED ON SET

Date: Tue, 26 Nov 2002 14:04:53 -0800 (PST)
From: "Gabe Kaplan" <gabe@gabekaplan.com>
Subject: The Ramsters
To: rlee@fnaws.org

Dear Mr. Lee,

As executive director of the Wild Sheep Foundation, I was hoping you might be able to help me.

The UPN Network and I will soon shoot a pilot called, "The Ramsters." Despite the name it's a comedy. It's about two buddies who personify the word "macho" and are always trying to outdo each other in every aspect of their lives.

I don't know if you folks out there at the Foundation know what the term "titles" means. The "titles" refer to the same scene you see every week at the opening of all television shows. In a comedy it's usually cute and funny stuff. We thought the "titles" of our new show, "The Ramsters," should depict our two protagonists on a mountain charging at each other and smashing heads. What do you think? Do you think it's a funny idea? Is it too much of a stretch to think that men could do this like sheep? Anything else the sheep do that you think is funny? Remember, "funny" is what we're looking for. Vulnerability is important also.

I know this is not your typical request. Also, the guys live in separate apartments on the same floor of a Chicago high rise. One of their downstairs neighbors is a lesbian and the doorman of the building is a religious fanatic. We are contractually bound to include these characters in the opening sequence. What would these two be doing (if they were behaving like sheep) while our guys are butting heads? Any ideas you have about this would also be greatly appreciated.

It's better to butt heads then hearts,

Gabe Kaplan
gabe@gabekaplan.com

PS I'm giving serious thought to changing the name of the show to, "Chicago Bighorns." Do you think that's better?

Date:	Sat, 30 Nov 2002 15:12:52 -0700
From:	"Ray Lee" <rlee@fnaws.org>
Subject:	Re: The Ramsters
To:	gabe@gabekaplan.com

Dear Mr. Kaplan:

I would suggest you go with the name "the ramsters" (it sounds something like "the honeymooners," a somewhat successful show, and less like an arena football team, the Chicago Bighorns!).

Personally, I think the premise is funny (and the mountain dew commercial was certainly popular).

The nice thing about animal behavior is that it is extremely popular right now as evidenced by the many nature shows. Wild sheep display many behavioral traits that could be cleverly adapted to humans - lesbians would be easy, religious fanatics a little more difficult. Off the top of my head I picture a lone ram sitting on the top of the mountain looking down on the warring machos - not too far removed from gurus, monks, and mystics.

Another nice thing about wild sheep is that it is possible to acquire considerable film footage to use in the title - ie., a few seconds of real sheep followed by the interspersion of your cast of characters.

I like the concept, let me know if I can help.

Ray Lee

BEATING WILT'S RECORD

Date:	Thu, 10 Apr 2003 21:06:19 -0700 (PDT)
From:	"Gabe Kaplan" <gabe@gabekaplan.com>
Subject:	Interesting Book Idea
To:	lyle@barricadebooks.com

Dear Mr. Stuart,

As you say on your website, you really do push the First Ammendment. I've read the Steve Wynn book and have been following its controversy. I'm also looking forward to "Celebrity Lies". I hope I'm not included in that one!

I have a project you might be interested in getting involved with. You could just review it when it's finished and see if you want to publish or get involved at the ground level and find me someone to write with. I can't do it alone. Here's the subject matter:

In 1991, after publishing his book, "A View From Above," Wilt Chamberlain was a guest on my sports radio show. Everybody, of course, was talking about his amazing claim that he had sex with 20,000 women. I was especially curious because I am known as quite a swordsman myself.

At age 17, I started my comedy career working as an MC in strip clubs. Many of the eager strippers I encountered became the first entries on my lifetime list. However, I did not really find my stroke until I began working the Playboy Clubs in the late '60s. To put it delicately, after four years on that circuit, I had one exhausted jimmy-jang. Then, of course, there was Vegas with all its showgirls and dancers and, in La La Land, there were many female perks available to the star of a hit sitcom. Then, of course, there was "The Mansion"...

Talking to Wilt after our interview, I estimated my lifetime total at well over 10,000. He jokingly said, "Well, I guess you're too old to catch me." Two months later my radio show was cancelled. "What am I going to do with the rest of my life," I wondered. I looked myself in the mirror and said, "Kappie, go for Wilt's record! When you buy the farm, what good is the silver medal?"

So, for the last eleven years I haven't worked very much at all. I spend all my time in pursuit of Wilt's record. At my current pace of two women a day, I will pass Wilt in September of next year. To be perfectly candid, most of the women in the last five years have been compensated (no repeats) and I was forced to purchase a penis pump in '98. This has not limited my output but has reduced the number of positions I'm able to assume comfortably.

At this point there's little fun involved, I'm just grinding it out to break Wilt's record. Out of my 20,000 women forty-two are recognizable names, including one member of the U.S. Senate.

I'm interested in having the book published after I pass the magic number next January. I figure it would take at least eight months to complete because of my encounters and nap schedule. I would want to be involved in the writing at all times. Let me know if you're interested.
Still counting,

Gabe Kaplan
gabe@gabekaplan.com

PS If I have to accept an asterisk because of the pump so be it.

Date:	Fri, 11 Apr 2003 13:02:10 -0400
From:	"Lyle Stuart" <lyle@barricadebooks.com>
Subject:	Your book
To:	gabe@gabekaplan.com

Amused to get your report. At the moment we're
arranging to publish a sequel to Running Scared.
That should cover our legal bills...

Regarding your project: Are you living in this
area? We'd have to have discussions of concept
and creating the work and this would be tough by
E-mail.

Lyle Stuart

Date: Fri, 11 Apr 2003 22:29:20 -0700 (PDT)
From: "Gabe Kaplan" <gabe@gabekaplan.com>
Subject: New Book... I Hate To Negotiate
To: lyle@barricadebooks.com

Lyle,

Thanks for your prompt reply. I live in Southern California but will be in Jersey in early May. I play each year in the annual Lazlo Sarducci Bocci Ball Tournament. If it looks like our working together is a possibility, I'd love to meet while I'm there.

Can you give me some indication of the best way to initially proceed? Doing business on the phone is bad for me, because I'm usually taken advantage of. I bought MCI's Neighborhood Plan from six different people. If I only lived in six different neighborhoods! Do I need an agent to deal with you? I hate to negotiate.

The writer I'm looking for would have to combine the salacious subject matter with a sense of humor. They would have to work around my bizarre schedule and remind me to take my pills. Does anybody come immediately to mind? I'm willing to get a little self-deprecating but on the other hand I do feel quite a sense of accomplishment. I'd want my collaborator to be impressed by my achievements, but not in awe. I'm completely open to working with a woman in a totally platonic and professional manner.

Your thoughts?

Gabe
gabe@gabekaplan.com

PS You'll be happy to know that while on trips, I'm usually totally celibate. I can't deal with the stress of traveling.

Date:	Sat, 12 Apr 2003 11:35:53 -0400
From:	"Lyle Stuart" <lyle@barricadebooks.com>
Subject:	Your book
To:	gabe@gabekaplan.com

I have an excellent writer in mind but am not
sure she's open to the project but will approach
her. She's a terrific writer with a marvelous
sense of humor.

At the moment taking advantage of you isn't a
high priority. We tend to treat authors fairly.
We pay nominal advances but otherwise offer a
fair contract. For example, the author of The
Sensuous Woman got a $1,500 advance and before
it was through, earned more than $2 million. But
all of this can be discussed in a realxed way at
our dinner.

There may be one extra needed from you. I
play poker at the Friars Club every two weeks
and am a loser too often. Maybe you can teach
me something about poker in exchange for my
professional knowledge of casino games!

Date: Mon, 14 Apr 2003 00:05:53 -0700 (PDT)
From: "Gabe Kaplan" <gabe@gabekaplan.com>
Subject: Re: Who's 20,001 Going To Be?
To: lyle@barricadebooks.com

Lyle,

I'm starting to give some thought as to who number 20,000 and number 20,001 should be. Is the author of "The Sensuous Woman" married? She'd be a natural for one of those spots. From what you've told me she's rich, but I won't charge her.

I rarely play poker anymore. Occasionally I do the color for the Vegas tournament on ESPN. Vegas is great because I know I'm not the only guy there with a penis pump.

Gabe

Date:	Wed, 21 May 2003 13:07:25 -0400
From:	"Lyle Stuart" <lyle@barricadebooks.com>
Subject:	Your best seller
To:	gabe@gabekaplan.com

Since you're not coming east, we'll come west!

From Memorial Day until June 1st, we'll be at a friends house in Beverly Hills. My cell phone is the direct way to reach me: 201-XXX-XXXX

Lyle Stuart

Date:	Sat, 24 May 2003 01:02:52 -0700 (PDT)
From:	"Gabe Kaplan" <gabe@gabekaplan.com>
Subject:	Competition Is Good!
To:	lyle@barricadebooks.com

Lyle:

I hadn't heard from you. Another publisher is also interested in my project. He says that now along with hard covers, they make audio versions of books and call them "Books On Tape." I would do the reading and we could get all 20,000 women to say how I was. Maybe a few thought there was something personal going on.

The Senator who was and still is married, has refused to be interviewed on tape. I guess she's being careful. You know politicians.

This might be a little more information than you care to know, but next week I'm moving off the pump to the latest three-piece self lubricating penile implant. Supposedly, it saves energy. It's been getting more and more difficult to keep up the two-a-days and I really want to be finished by next September. After that, I'll never want to have sex again (at least in this lifetime).

Gabe
gabe@gabekaplan.com

PS If I do the book with someone else, I'll still give you a free poker lesson when I'm in NY.

Date:	Tue, 27 May 2003 13:20:50 -0400
From:	"Lyle Stuart" <lyle@barricadebooks.com>
Subject:	Competition
To:	gabe@gabekaplan.com

We don't compete in terms of advances. I thought
you came to us because Dr. Albert Ellis and I
launched the world-wide sexual revolution in
1958 with Sex Without Guilt, The Art & Science
of Love; Sex & The Single Man, etc. I followed
these with the million copy seller The Marriage
Art and the 13-million copy The Sensuous Woman
and the 6+ million copy seller The Sensuous Man.

Peter Mayle flew from London for his Where Did I
Come From? and chose us above BIG money offers
from Random House and Doubleday. We gave him a
$3,000 advance and then did what I said we'd
do: we made the book a 2-million copy seller
in the states and sold translation rights in
14 countries. In Germany they published six
regional dialect editions.

Since that isn't why you came to Barricade, I
won't try to dissuade you from going for the
larger advance. What we had to offer you was a
ghost who could get just the right balance of
information, titillation and humor.

Thanks for your offer of a poker lesson. I've
lost for 12 months in that once-every=two=weeks
poker game at the Friars.

Good luck with the book...

Lyle

Date:	Sun, 29 Jun 2003 20:34:55 -0400
From:	"Lyle Stuart" <lyle@barricadebooks.com>
Subject:	Ho Ho Ho!
To:	gabe@gabekaplan.com

Ho Ho Ho! So now we've got a book about the guy who owned Plato's Retreat and claims to have been laid 20,000 times. He came to us independently so you'll have to work harder.

Lyle

Date:	Mon, 30 Jun 2003 23:06:54 -0700 (PDT)
From:	"Gabe Kaplan" <gabe@gabekaplan.com>
Subject:	Ho Ho Ho! I'm disappointed
To:	lyle@barricadebooks.com

Lyle:

Well, my good friend, you've upset me so much I couldn't complete the act with the two women scheduled for today. They had to work extra hard and, despite their efforts, are not even going to make the list. No penetration, no listing, that's my rule. It's cold, but I am driven not only by passion, but integrity as well .

Let's examine these two books. One is by an unknown man who participated in countless orgies, not even knowing the names of most of the women he had sex with. The second one is by a parental, beloved TV star who just happens to be a sex addict and has slept with some very important women among his 20,000. No orgies! Which one would you buy?

Why do you start your letter by saying "Ho Ho Ho!", are you passing some subtle comment about the caliber of women, I've been seeing lately?

You still get the NY poker lesson.

Gabe

SEVERAL MONTHS AFTER MY CORRESPONDENCE WITH MR. STUART HAD CEASED, HE PUT OUT HIS ANNUAL COMPANY NEWSLETTER TO THE PUBLISHING INDUSTRY. I WAS ITEM NUMBER 3, AS SEEN BELOW.

3

I knew who Gabe Kaplan was, although I confess that I've never watched his sitcom "Welcome Back, Kotter." I also knew that he was a winner in a poker tournament. That's about all I knew.

He approached me to publish a book about his sexual contacts with women. He was striving to break the record of Wilt Chamberlain, who claimed to have slept with 10,000.

It could have been an amusing book if written with the right mix of humor. But before we could come to terms, he asked if I would match an offer he'd received from a west coast publisher who deals largely in audio cassettes. I explained that our company specializes in controversy and we don't get into bidding wars—and that was that. The west coast company has since gone bankrupt.

GREECE IS THE WORD

Date:	Tue, 11 Feb 2003 20:29:57 -0800 (PST)
From:	"Gabe Kaplan" <gabe@gabekaplan.com>
Subject:	Lighting Olympic Torch
To:	mediade@athens2004.gr

Dear Athens Olympic Committee,

How's it going with all the preparations? Are you on schedule? Someone told me - I think it was Leon Spinks - that the velodrome may not be built in time. I'm sure that's just another one of those bogus, pre-Olympic rumors. I don't believe it. I'm pretty confident your country can overcome many problems and give the world one of the best Summer Olympics we've seen.

Deciding who lights the Olympic torch is a major factor in the success of all that follows. I humbly believe that if I were to be assigned the honor, it would get things going in the right direction. I'm sure you're aware that I'm one of the beloved international television celebrities of all time. However, you may not know that I was also quite an athlete in my day - not Olympic caliber, but close. Anyone who's seen "Battle of the Network Stars" knows of my athletic prowess.

The Muhammad Ali surprise worked for Atlanta and a celebrity of equal world-wide notoriety would be perfect for Greece. Yours is the oldest civilization on earth, requiring someone who symbolizes classic dignity evocative of the Spartan culture.

I do not expect any financial remuneration beyond first-class accommodations and travel for my manservant, James Fitzwilliam, and me. This arrangement would be in place, of course, for the entire length of the Games.

Greece is the word,

Gabe Kaplan
gabe@gabekaplan.com

Date:	Fri, 21 Mar 2003 15:35:25 +0200
From:	"Protekdikou Aikaterini" <AProte@athens2004.com>
Subject:	Lighting Olympic Torch
To:	gabe@gabekaplan.com

Dear Mr. Kaplan:

Thank you for your offer of participation in the Opening Ceremonies of the Games of the XXVIIIth Olympiad in Athens, 2004. However we cannot accept your proposal for many reasons. The role of the Flame in the Olympic ceremonies is an important connection between the modern Games and their origins in Ancient Greece. Because the flame is held in such high esteem it is treated with reverence and respect. Because of this the role of final torchbearer is reserved for someone who has exemplified the principles of Olympism with pride and dignity. We are sure that if you were familiar with the history of Greece and the Olympic Games this would become clear to you.
In addition, in all of the Olympic Games that took place in the United States of America (as listed below)
1960 - LAKE PLACID - Dr Charles Morgan Ker
1984 - LOS ANGELES - Wafer Johnson
1996 - ATLANTA - Muhammad Ali
2002 - SALT LAKE - National Hokey Team (gold medalists in 1960)
the last torchbearer to light the cauldron in the stadium was an American citizen. We plan to do so in the Athens 2004 Olympic Games.
We thank you for your interest with best wishes for success in your show business career.

Sincerely,
ATHANASSIOS KRITSINELIS
Manager of Greek Torch Relay

5 ARTS AND CRAPS

Date: Thu, 08 May 2003 14:10:13 -0700 (PDT)
From: "Gabe Kaplan" <gabe@gabekaplan.com>
Subject: New Exciting Summer Camp for 2004
To: camptrip@campadvisors.com

Dear Ms. Shiffman and Ms Borodkin:

Permit me to introduce myself. My name is Gabe Kaplan. I think I've developed a unique and groundbreaking concept and I hope you'll be as excited about it as I am. Since you are experts in the field of summer camps, I would appreciate it if you would give me your unbiased opinion about this type of camp and whether or not it will be successful. Also, would you recommend it to interested parties?

On June 24th of 2004 we will kick-off the inaugural season of "The Gabe Kaplan Co-Ed Summer Gaming Camp for Children 12-17." Located on ten spacious acres on the outskirts of Parump, Nevada, the camp will offer a comprehensive program of electives like no other.

On several occasions as a parent I've gone through the process of seeking out the right camp for my child, only to be disappointed because I couldn't find a camp for youngsters interested in gaming.

At **GKSGC** we'll offer all the typical sports (except swimming and baseball), arts and crafts, and theatrical productions. In addition, for our campers, I'll feature a slew of activities I don't believe are offered anywhere else.

They include but are not limited to: Sports Betting, Poker, Craps, and Black Jack Skills, An Introduction to The Nation's Racetracks, The Pitfalls of Bingo and Slots, and, most importantly, How To Bet with Your Head, Not Over It.

We might raise some eyebrows, but for realistic people such as myself, **GKSGC** offers an alternative to parents and campers interested in the subject matter.

Let me know what you think and I hope I can count on your seal of approval. If you run across anybody who's looking for this type of summer experience for his or her child, please let me know.

Kumbaya,

Gabe Kaplan
gabe@gabekaplan.com

PS Real money is never used in any of our activities.

Date:	Thu, 22 May 2003 16:36:35 -0400
From:	"Beverly Shiffman" <camptrip@gis.net>
Subject:	Gambling Camp
To:	gabe@gabekaplan.com

What are the odds that anyone would want a kids camp with no swimming, no baseball (which I know is a passion of yours...I read the website) and a plethora of gambling skills? Sounds like every mother's dream!

Starting up a camp like this will really be shooting craps, but who knows...stranger things have happened. Are cigars and those green eye shades part of the tuition? And just where is Pahrump, Nevada? Is it near Dorten and Yenumsville?

We have been in business for almost 35 years and have had requests that You wouldn't believe, requests that would curl your hair or in your case straighten your hair. But never has any kid or parent asked for a Gambling camp, but with the economy as it is, maybe this is a better route to financial success than college.

Good luck with GKSGC. Roll the dice and see what comes up. Maybe you'll be lucky.

Bev and Diane

6 HALAQUIN-GABIO

Date: Thu, 08 May 2003 11:52:00 -0700 (PDT)
From: "Gabe Kaplan" <gabe@gabekaplan.com>
Subject: Public Relations Question for Katherine Orr
To: public_relations@harlequin.ca

Dear Ms.Orr,

My new wife, Rona, and my adult daughter, Davayah, are big fans of
your romance novels. They exchange them and discuss them all the
time. Davayah is actually three months older than Rona so, although
I might have some snow on the roof, there's still a fire somewhere.
Women of all ages can sense that about me. Although I'm not the
best looking guy in the world my sexuality is obvious to the gals.

As you more than anyone must know, some women prefer older men.
A few of your novels are about these types of relationships. How
about using me on the jacket of one of your novels with this theme of
May-December romance? (Enclosed find a current picture.) It might
be a kick having a semi-recognizable face gracing one of your book
covers. It also might sell more books. You just pay me what you pay
your regular models.

Rona and Davayah would go bananas
when that book hits the stands. I
wouldn't dream of telling them
beforehand. It would kill the whole
surprise.

Let me know what you think,

Gabe Kaplan

PS You can airbrush any photo
of me as much as you want

Date:	Thu, 08 May 2003 16:08:33 -0400
From:	"Katherine Orr" <Katherine_Orr@Harlequin.ca>
Subject:	Harlequin book cover
To:	gabe@gabekaplan.com

Is this really you? Please call me on my direct line if it is...416-XXX-XXXX. I apologize for the skepticism but you can imagine how many requests we get to be on our covers.....Regards, Katherine

---

Katherine Orr
Vice President Public Relations
Harlequin Enterprises Limited
225 Duncan Mill Road
Toronto, Ontario
M3B 3K9
Phone: (416) XXX XXXX
Fax: (416) XXX XXXX

Date: Mon, 20 Jan 2003 13:18:27 -0800 (PST)
From: "Gabe Kaplan" <gabe@gabekaplan.com>
Subject: The First Idiot Letters
To: prosa@pclsys.net

Dear Paul,

It seems you're the guy that started a whole new series of letter books. There was "The Lazlo Letters," then nothing I can remember for twenty years.

I have some information with which you may be familiar. If not, I'm sure you'll find it fascinating.

The first person to write funny letters and elicit responses was Lord Byron. Byron was a notorious drunk and practical joker. There is a famous story of him giving a bible to his publisher and substituting the publisher's name for Barabbas's. He also published an anonymous satire, "English Bards and Scotch Reviewers." These facts are common knowledge.

Little known and lost to history is the fact that between 1811 and 1815 Byron got off on writing silly letters to merchants and acclaimed people of the day. He used the name Byron Grey and had the letters sent from a friend's address on the outskirts of London. For years the letters were a great amusement to his peers, including Shelley and Keats.

I don't want to assume you're interested, but if you are, I can e-mail you the few I have and tell you what I've heard about the story surrounding the letters.

Enjoyed your book.

Gabe Kaplan
gabe@gabekaplan.com

Gabe (THE Gabe Kaplan?),

The Lord Byron stuff sounds fantastic. I LOVED the "Bible submission!"

I would love to hear/read more about Byron.. thank you very much for offering.

Some of the best silly letter books were written by James C. Wade, like "P.S. My Bush Pig's Name Is Boris." Brilliantly twisted. Have you seen em?

Probably the best seller was "Letters From a Nut," which came out right after mine but was heavily promoted on all the major talk shows by his friend, Jerry Seinfeld. Grrrrrrrrr........

I think you might chortle at my website... www.idiot-ink.com

If you are indeed comedian Gabe Kaplan (I did 8 years on the road), I Would be honored to meet you. Hell, even if you're not! Where do you live? What are you working on?

Please send an XL T-shirt.

Regards,
Paul "Paul" Rosa

Paul,

Thanks for the tip on Wade's books. I've already ordered "Bush's Pig."

In answer to your questions, yes it's me, I live in Los Angeles, and I'll be hosting Celebrity Scratch & Sniff this summer on Fox.

I still do a little standup, but concentrate mostly on business interests. It's surprising we never ran in to each other, we probably worked a lot of the same clubs. If you're in L.A. we should get together and swap war stories.

Here are two of the Byron Grey letters. Hope you enjoy them. I have one more, but have not located it yet. It's to Henry Hastings Plumbers, and it's hysterical. I'll keep looking. The ones I'm sending are to a renowned portrait artist and a cheese merchant.

There's a chap in England who claims to have fifteen, but refuses to share them with anybody. To use your words, "Grrrrrrrrrrr...."

After you read these, I'll fill you in on what I've been told regarding their history. I have these two in their original form also. If you would like to see them, I can scan and send them.

Show them to whomever you want but please don't post them on the Internet.

I'll also be sending a young rabbit to show you how much I liked your book.

Gabe "Gabe" Kaplan

Dear Sir Thomas Lawrence, By way of introduction, I am
Byron Grey, a gentleman farmer from Tottenham north. Some
of your highly esteemed brethren have selected our community
for country house. Your humble servant had privilege to view
your artistry at the estate of Clarence Dowling. You, sir, are
one of the great portrait masters of London, if indeed not the
entire of Europe. I do not mean this exordium as a threat to
induce you to comply with my unusual request, but merely
as a sincere compliment having seen your work. I propose a
London visit three weeks hence, to commission a portrait of
my wife, daughter and me standing aside our prize sheep. The
particular sheep shall pose no behavioural threat to your studio.
One might properly inquire as to why I don't employ one of
several accomplished portrait artists in my immediate region.
This sheep is blood-tied, and your masterful brush captures
family like no other. This portrait is intended for the hearth of
the principal cottage. In future, after Agnes has departed our
earth, we who remain can gaze and remember times passed.
If you have the least doubt of my integrity or feel you may
compromise your good reputation, do not hesitate in your
refusal. I selfishly hold hope you will not feel your esteem
diminished by the painting of one head of livestock. I offer to
you double the standard portrait fee and am sending a young
rabbit for your troubles.

Sincerely, with good thoughts to you my gifted Sir,

Byron Grey

Dear Paxton and Whitfield, I write to explain a foolish circumstance, your discretion is sought. The mother of my wife, has taken up residence with us two months now. She is Mrs. Parkins of Kent. Regrettable she has three unpardonable flaws, imperfections rare for someone of social register. She is strong in her opinions in the way of world affairs, yet uninformed as to the political process itself; In addition and without shame, she boasts of her association with jockeys, gamblers, boxers, authors, parsons and poets. These traits alone chew the cud off my reconciliation with any woman. Most egregious, however, is her penchant for feeding on the most disagreeable brand of Kent cheeses. Each night the appallingly wicked aromas her body produces from these cheeses fill our property. If I were to confide in you that these odors, without help of sword, lance, or shield would be of strength to halt the king's army, this would not be a stretch of circumstance. The worst of nightmares has occurred. Many nights, if I thought I could acquit myself, I would have bludgeoned the poor women. I beg you good and reputable Cheese Mongers to advise me a substitute goods that would be similar in taste without producing such heinous results. How my nostrils will rejoice should this be accomplished. I am sending a young rabbit for your trouble.

Believe me, my dear Sirs, yours ever sincerely,

Byron Grey

Date:	Fri, 07 Feb 2003 23:27:45 -0500
From:	"Paul Rosa" <prosa@pcisys.net>
Subject:	Re: Sending two Byron Grey Letters
To:	gabe@gabekaplan.com

Very nice. Thanks, Gabe!

Would love to hear more and see scans, and shall
certainly NOT post on internet!

I'd love to meet you sometime and will certainly
let you know if I'm LA bound. Please do the same
if headed to NYC!

-Paul

Date: Thu, 05 Jun 2003 12:19:34 -0700 (PDT)
From: "Gabe Kaplan" <gabe@gabekaplan.com>
Subject: Byron, Letter Books and Extra-Large T-Shirts
To: prosa@pcisys.net

Paul,

Sorry for the delay. Here are copies of the two original Byron letters. I still can't find the third one. I've been on the road for most of the last few months and it's good to be back in LA. No stock this summer. Fiddler, Guys, and Cats will have to get by without me.

Since I have my whole summer free, I was looking for an interesting project to tackle. What do you think of this idea? A silly letter book from a known personality. I could write to companies, hotels, and individuals with ridiculous requests. The difference of course being that they would know who I am and probably treat my letters with kid gloves (or in some cases boxing gloves).

Any feedback you give me would be appreciated. I wouldn't be stepping on your turf, would I? Are there a lot of legal issue involved? Can you just publish any response you receive?

Before you ask, the extra large t-shirts have been ordered and should be arriving any day now.

Gabe
gabe@gabekaplan.com

Dear Sir Thomas Lawrence, By way of introduction, I am Byron Grey, a gentleman farmer from Totterham north. Some of your highly esteemed brethren have selected our community for country houses. Your humble servant had privilege to view your artistry at the estate of Clarence Dowling. You, sir, are one of the great portrait masters of London, if indeed not the entire of Europe. I do not mean this encomium as a threat to induce you to comply with my unusual request, but merely as a sincere compliment having seen your work. I propose a visit to London three weeks hence, February second, to commission a portrait of my wife, daughter and I standing aside our prize sheep. The particular sheep shall pose no behavioural threat to your studio. One might properly inquire as to why I don't employ one of several accomplished portrait artists in my immediate regions. This sheep is blood-tied, and your masterful brush captures family like no other. This portrait is intended for the hearth of the principal cottage. In future, after Agnes has departed our earth, we who remain can gage and remember times passed. If you have the least doubt of my integrity or feel you may compromise your good reputation, do not hesitate in your refusal. I selfishly hold hope you will not feel your esteem diminished by the painting of one head of livestock. I offer to you double the standard portrait fee and am sending a young rabbit for your troubles.

      Sincerely, with good thoughts to you,
      my gifted sir,
      Byron Grey

Dear Karston and Whitfield, to wish to explain a foolish circumstance, your discretion is sought. The mother of my wife has taken up residence with us two months now.

She is Mrs. Perkins of Kent. Regrettable she has three unpardonable flaws, imperfections rare for someone of social register.

She is strong in her opinions in the way of world affairs, yet uninformed as to the political process itself; in addition and without shame, she boasts of her association with jockeys, gardeners, boxers, authors, parsons and poets. These traits alone then do cut off my reconciliation with any female.

Most egregious, however, is her penchant for feeding on the most disagreeable brand of Kent cheeses. Each night the appallingly wicked aromas her body produces from these cheeses fill our property. If I were to confide in you that these odors, without the help of sword, lance or shield would be strength to halt the King's army, this would not be a stretch of circumstance.

The worst of nightmares have occurred. Many nights, if I thought I could acquit myself, I would have bludgeoned the poor woman.

I beg you good and reputable cheese mongers to advise me a substitute goods that would be similar in taste without producing such poisonous results. Then my nostrils will rejoice should this be accomplished.

I am sending a young rabbit for your trouble.

Believe me, my dear sirs, yours ever sincerely,

Lyon Grey

Date:	Thu, 05 Jun 2003 22:07:29 -0400
From:	"Paul Rosa" <prosa@pcisys.net>
Subject:	Letter Book
To:	gabe@gabekaplan.com

Thanks, Gabe.

I like the idea of letters FROM a celebrity although there have been a LOT of letter books in recent years, the most successful coming from Jerry Seinfeld's pal, Ted Nancy.

I think it would be funny if you tried to get parts for characters clearly better suited for Brad Pitt, Tom Cruise, or even Julia Roberts! Or submit crappy screenplay ideas, etc.

Regarding publishing legalities, that's kind of a lengthy topic. Do you mind calling me at 212-XXX-XXXX.

Paul

Date:	Fri, 06 Jun 2003 01:58:46 -0700 (PDT)
From:	"Gabe Kaplan" <gabe@gabekaplan.com>
Subject:	Re: Letter Book
To:	prosa@pcisys.net

Paul,

It's a good idea to submit myself for Brad Pitt-type parts. The only problem is they won't even consider me for Gabe Kaplan-type parts at this point. So I don't even think I would get much of a rejection.

What about if I wrote a letter to Ted L. Nancy saying I wanted to translate his books into Inuit? I could tell him the Eskimos just love silly stuff and have been deprived of his humor too long. The Arctic Circle is demanding "Letters From A Nut"!

Before I bother you about the legalities, let me make sure I have the time and correct frame of mind to tackle this project. Did you ever feel weird sending any of the letters? Sometimes I think it's a great and other times the whole idea embarrasses me.

Gabe
gabe@gabekaplan.com

Date:	Fri, 06 Jun 2003 14:03:44 -0400
From:	"Paul Rosa" <prosa@pcisys.net>
Subject:	Re: Letter Book
To:	gabe@gabekaplan.com

The idea of messing with those who've messed with others is groovy!

I *always* enjoyed sending the letters and took it as a personal challenge to get answers to every one of them. I would keep writing until they answered and succeeded with about 168 out of 170 letters I wrote!

But you can always begin writing and see how you feel.

Do you think many people will assume "Gabe Kaplan" is really someone else and that may mess up the project in some way?

Call anytime.

-Paul

Date:	Sat, 07 Jun 2003 22:42:47 -0400
From:	"Paul Rosa" <prosa@pcisys.net>
Subject:	Re: Letter Book
To:	gabe@gabekaplan.com

Gabe,

Can you please send e-mail me the Byron letter texts (not originals) again? I can't find em!

Thanks,
Paul

Date: Sun, 08 Jun 2003 21:07:49 -0700 (PDT)
From: "Gabe Kaplan" <gabe@gabekaplan.com>
Subject: Here's Byron
To: prosa@pcisys.net

Paul:

Here again are the texts of the two Byron letters. It's not you —
everybody keeps losing them. I still can't find the funniest one (to
Henry Hastings, Plummers). Maybe it's Byron's ghost trying to play
havoc with the proof of how silly he was. We should write a script
called "Byrongeist" where he terrorizes a Long Island community
because some high school English teacher finds out about his Byron
Grey letters.

You didn't comment on the embarrassment factor in sending *your*
letters. In any case it would be a little different for me, people might
take offense at my putting them on. Then if I can't publish without
permission, it might be hard to come by.

I also thought about possibly doing them through e-mail. It's would
be faster and easier. Plus, you don't need to buy stamps. I realize I
would lose the outgoing and incoming letterheads and that's a big
part of these kind of books. Any opinions?

Gabe
gabe@gabekaplan.com

Date:	Mon, 9 Jun 2003 13:28:59 -0400
From:	"Paul Rosa" <prosa@pcisys.net>
Subject:	Re: Here's Byron
To:	gabe@gabekaplan.com

Thanks, Gabe.

I wasn't the slightest bit embarrassed by writing the letters (is that what you mean?). Legally, I think we "technically" needed permission to print the incoming letters but the Doubleday lawyers determined the risks to be virtually zero. And I've never heard of any legal action against any of the letter writers.

So we didn't ask permission. It is my understanding that if we asked permission and it was denied and we *still* printed them then *that* could be trouble.

Yes, e-mail is a good idea. I had considered doing an e-mail letter book too. Here's something good about e-mail: You can quickly e-mail several copies of the same letter to various, similar organizations and keep only the best response for the book. I did that with letters. For instance if I wished to write to a candy bar company I'd send a letter to 3-4 of them.

Best,
Paul

MAD SKILLZ

Date: Tue, 11 Nov 2003 15:26:21 -0800 (PST)
From: "Gabe Kaplan" <gabe@gabekaplan.com>
Subject: Gabe Kaplan Raps
To: david.saslow@interscoped.com

Dear Mr. Saslow,

Whaddup, dog? Me myself, I'm keepin' it real. 'Course, at my age, I'm startin' to have issues wit makin' ends. You dig? I'm ol' school. Last night I was chillin' wit some hotties at my crib, all g'd up, drinkin' forty dogs, firin' up a blunt and this ho be lookin' at my dukey rope. I said, "bitch don't be lookin' at my bling bling. If you wanna bag up on my bone, you gots to axe me straight up." Bitch says to me, "homey please, if you wanna get busy wit yo jimmy in my jenny, you gots to front the flow." I said, "Damn, this bitch be a sack chasin', Mrs. Howell III. I said, I ain't lookin' for none of dat dugout."

So, David, what do you think of my grasp of the street lingo? Reason I ask; I'm attempting to give my career more of a contemporary "flava." I've been in the business over forty years and I've noticed recently that audiences are tiring of my middle-of-the-road shtick. What can I do, I thought to myself? Everywhere you turn you see people wearing over-sized clothing and jiving to the latest hip-hop rhymes. Even white performers are getting into the act, what with Eminem, The Beastie Boys, and Vanilla Ice. All the white guys try to act black and talk Ebonics. Why not me? As a force in the record business, and the man behind Fred Durst, you're the first person I'm contacting.

I've written a rap song called, "Da Shit Be Different If I Was Black." (See below) This song could kick off my new "playa-type" act. I'd like you to be the one who produces it. Do you think people will accept this from me and would you be interested in publishing it?

I'm swayze,

Gabe Kaplan
Gabe@gabekaplan.com

"Da Shit Be Different If I Was Black"

Tryin' to get by on mailbox money
But it ain't enough bank to keep a honey
Peeps in da house ain't wit my shiz nit
I'm barely hangin' on in show biz'nit
Brothas today be getting all de props
Playas look at me and call me "ol' Pops"
They say the muthafucka once had it goin'
But holes in da ozone is all he showin'

I ONCE WAS DA MAN, BUT NOW I'M WACK
DA SHIT BE DIFFERENT IF I WAS BLACK

I wanna get down like I was new
Smokin' boats and bombs with my bitches and crew
I wanna see my ass on the WB
Not some peckerwood show on ABC
Cause if I get a shot to do my thing
Homies be blinded by my bling bling bling

I ONCE WAS DA MAN, BUT NOW I'M WACK
DA SHIT BE DIFFERENT IF I WAS BLACK

Clowns today, their gags are all stock
But I'm so funny, I get a laugh from yo cock,
So hop this train and take the ride of yo life
Be like buggin' on acid with Mr. Barney Fife
Transmogrification is what I'm about
And if you don't like it, YOU CAN GET THE FUCK OUT.

I ONCE WAS DA MAN, BUT NOW I'M WACK
DA SHIT BE DIFFERENT IF I WAS BLACK

Date:	Mon, 17 Nov 2003 13:25:31 -0800
From:	"Saslow, David" <david.saslow@interscoped.com>
Subject:	Gabe Kaplan Raps
To:	gabe@gabekaplan.com

Gabe,

Your skillz are nice!

-David

Date:	Sun, 06 Apr 2003 22:43:49 -0700 (PDT)
From:	"Gabe Kaplan" <gabe@gabekaplan.com>
Subject:	American Celebrity Cossack Dancer Extraordinaire
To:	Alex@cossack.com.au

Dear Alex,

Starting June 15th, I will be in Perth for at least a week. Would it be possible for me to audition for the Ukrainian Cossack Dancers during that period?

My dancing exploits (and high-pitched laugh) are quite familiar to everybody in the Southern California Ukrainian community. Don't think I might be too old until you see me dance. They call me "Bubka bez polius".

I also have some authentic costumes (men's and women's) that might be unfamiliar even to an afficionado like yourself. You'll love them!

Here's the bad part: If you want to hire me, I could only work 2 to 3 months per year, as I still have some acting commitments. I'm playing Sheridan Whiteside in "Dinner" this whole summer.

Vidannyy Vam,

Gabe Kaplan
gabe@gabekaplan.com

PS After you see me dance, we can talk about billing and compensation. I'm so bad at that anyway.

Date:	Mon, 07 Apr 2003 13:54:00 +0800
From:	"Alex" <Alex@cossack.com.au>
Subject:	Re: American Celebrity Cossack Dancer Extraordinaire
To:	gabe@gabekaplan.com

Gabe

We are an amateur group so it is not possible to hire any dancers.

Thank you for your email though and enjoy your stay in Perth.

Alex

Date: Mon, 07 Apr 2003 23:39:06 -0700 (PDT)
From: "Gabe Kaplan" <gabe@gabekaplan.com>
Subject: Re: Thanks For Reply And Offer!
To: Alex@cossack.com.au

Dear Alex,

Thank you so much for your speedy reply and your interest in having me dance with your troupe. I understand that there is no financial remuneration, so all we would have to do is agree on the billing for the one or two performances I'm involved in. How much rehearsal do you feel would be required?

Sometimes, at the end of my performances over here, the rest of the troupe leaves the stage and I do a few jokes, mostly in English. There are a few with salty Ukrainian punch lines but I would feel the crowd out and know whether or not they would be appropriate. Did you know that "farmer's daughter" jokes (fermer donka zhart) were started in the Ukraine? They were told by the Poles, during the early 17th century, right before liberation? They used to be quite an insult but by now people have forgotten and everybody enjoys them.

I called my friends in Perth and told them about your offer. They're all excited and, of course, want free tickets. I said I'd have to abide by whatever your policy was.

Do My Zustrichaty,

Gabe
gabe@gabekaplan.com

Date:	Wed, 09 Apr 2003 11:03:53 +0800
From:	"Alex" <Alex@cossack.com.au>
Subject:	Re: Thanks For Reply And Offer!
To:	gabe@gabekaplan.com

Gabe

I am sorry if my email caused any confusion
but I do not consider our group would be able
to utilise your performances - we would not
and do not pay performers and in any event do
not know if there would be any performances in
the relevant period. You may want to email Mr.
Mykytiuk who is the President of the Hromada
here as he may be interested in utilising your
ability for a performance. His email is:
myk@ukraina.com

Alex

Date: Fri, 23 May 2003 15:16:48 -0700 (PDT)
From: "Gabe Kaplan" <gabe@gabekaplan.com>
Subject: Dear Mr. Mykytiuk, I am writing this to you.
To: myk@ukraina.com

Dear Mr. Mykytiuk,

Alex is very excited about the possibility of my doing some Cossack dancing when I'm in Perth starting June, 15th. He enthusiastically suggested I contact you. It would be a shame for me to be in Australia for over a week and not be able to do any dancing or display some of my award winning costumes.

For a long time I've been trying to experiment combining the dancing we love with another completely different style of hoofing, something that no one would expect. River Dance did this with black tap dancers and it was very effective.

The southern California Ukrainian community is traditional and they haven't wanted to experiment. How about if you got some Aborigine folk dancers for the week I was there and we tried to see if we could combine them with Ukrainian Cossack? We could call it The Original Australian Uaboriginals. I'll take some pictures with my digital camera, and maybe I can drum up some interest in the States when I get back. I've already spoken to Steve Lawrence and Edie Gormet and they think this could be the start of something big.

Please let me know your thoughts. I've enclosed a picture with one of my oldest costumes. Looking forward to meeting you and working together.

Do Pobachennia, Tovarysh

Gabe Kaplan

PS How do you like being Australijs'kjs?

HAVE JOKES, WILL TRAVEL

Date:	Tue, 29 Apr 2003 08:51:09 -0700 (PDT)
From:	"Rachel and Dave Meth" <daurache@methado.com>
Subject:	Big fan
To:	gabe@gabekaplan.com

My wife's birthday is coming up in May...she was
a huge fan of Welcome Back Kotter (as was I, but
I liked you even more as Groucho).....can you
tell me if and how it would be possible to get
a personalized autograph picture of you....it
would make her day very special

Thanks so much

David Meth

Thu, 01 May 2003 00:28:19 -0700 (PDT)
From: "Gabe Kaplan" <gabe@gabekaplan.com>
Subject: My Pleasure!
To: daurache@methado.com

Dave,

I would be happy to send your wife an autographed black & white 8"x10" glossy photo. It's $10.00 signed, $5.00 unsigned. Color is $20.00 with a personalized signature. I'm actually running a special this week: A signed b&w photo, a Mr. Kotter key chain and a Gabe Kaplan mouse pad — all for the unbelievable low price of $25.00. Believe me Dave, I'm not making much on this. I'm just trying to make my fans happy.

On occasion, I have been hired by husbands to fly in for parties and surprise the birthday gal with a personal appearance. Would you be interested in something like that? You can use me in a variety of ways: I can kibbitz, I can act like a friend of the family, or here's another suggestion that's getting very popular — we can roast Rachel. Friends and family are the roasters and I'm the emcee. You give me some tidbits of information and we make it as clean or as racy as you'd like.

Think about it. All that's required is airfare, ground transportation and a reasonable financial honorarium (some of which goes to charity). You can put me up at a hotel but I'd be perfectly willing to stay at your house. I enjoy a large breakfast, which must include fresh fruit, an egg white spinach omelette, whole wheat toast and brewed coffee.

Let me know what I can do you for.

Gabe
gabe@gabekaplan.com

PS There's a picture of Groucho and myself, which I would throw in for free if you decide to do the roast.

Date:	Thu, 01 May 2003 10:41:27 -0700 (PDT)
From:	"Rachel and Dave Meth" <daurache@methado.com>
Subject:	Re: My Pleasure!
To:	gabe@gabekaplan.com

I love the roast idea!...unfortunately, having just bought her a new car for her upcoming birthday, I am a little tapped out at this point...out of curiousity, how much is the cost for your honorarium? (if you threw in Travolta, I could probably get my mom and sisters to pony up!)..and would you also join my buddies and me for a night of poker? (that would probably double the honorarium)

I need the address to send for the color picture..I'll let you know about the roast! Thanks for your response

David

Date: Sun, 04 May 2003 21:48:07 -0700 (PDT)
From: "Gabe Kaplan" <gabe@gabekaplan.com>
Subject: Honorariums?
To: daurache@methado.com

Dave,

Sorry for not answering sooner but I'm just returning from a roast in South Carolina. The woman involved was a 75 year-old Irish Traveler. Those folks know how to party! I don't need any siding so I hope this money order is good.

Let me know about your roast as soon as possible. May dates are filling up fast. In the meantime, send me your address and I'll send Rachel a free picture. Believe me Dave, I'm not making any money on the free picture.

The honorarium is whatever the family can afford. Only a dishonorable cad would dictate the price of an honorarium. Throw out a figure and we'll run it up the flagpole. I assume your comment about Travolta was a joke. Then again, Tiger Woods plays golf and has lunch with people for mega bucks. If you're serious about John I could make some inquiries.

I also sell Gabe Kaplan chips and playing cards for your poker game. Can you meet my breakfast requirements if we agree on all the other particulars for the roast?

Best to you and Rach,

Gabe
gabe@gabekaplan.com

Date:	Mon, 19 May 2003 14:25:48 -0700 (PDT)
From:	"Rachel and Dave Meth" <daurache@methado.com>
Subject:	Re: Honorariums?
To:	gabe@gabekaplan.com

Dear Gabe

Sorry it took so long to write back.....

My wife and I are very excited to see you tonite
on the ABC special....we saw the clip of you and
Barbarino....but whatever happened to Carvelli and
Judy Borden? (Carvelli was every kid that beat
me up for my lunch money..and I think every high
school had a Judy Borden..I know mine had about 20
of them, as a matter of fact, I think Judy Borden
is really my next door neighbor.)

My address is xxxxxxxxxxx...I stand by my promise to
send you a check for $25.00 for the color picture or
whatever else it costs(you can give it to charity if
you like)...we are already saving money for both a
future roast and a round of poker

Regards, David Meth

KAPLAN'S LOG: STAR DATE 2003.5

May 20, 2003

RE: Gabe Kaplan

Dear Harriet,

E! Entertainment Television aired a six-part series back in December of 2002 called "Star Dates." The show was an instant hit with our viewers and received a great deal of press from shows such as "Good Morning America" and "Howard Stern."

The premise of the show is to take a celebrity and cast two blind dates for them over a two evening period. Our cameras would then follow them on the dates & at the end of each date the celebrity would then talk about the date itself and what she or he *"did" or" didn't"* like about the person. We are very careful in "casting" the dates for our Celebrity guests, and go to great lengths to make them compatible. Since the show did so well ratings wise, we are coming back with another 13 episodes of "Star Dates" which will air in the summer of 2003.

We would like to make an offer to GABE KAPLAN to be one of our celebrity guests.

We are paying our celebrity guest a total of $4,000 for the two dates we arrange. This would be over a two evening period.

We take care of planning the date. Best of all we can talk about what our celebrity is currently promoting. We are currently in production through June.

E! is currently seen in over 80 million homes domestically, as well as internationally in mo than 120 countries, reaching 400 million homes worldwide.

Please let me know if there is interest on Gabe's behalf to be a celebrity guest. The show is all in fun and we really don't expect anymore to fall in love, but just have a good time, gets lots of press and get compensation as well. My direct line is 323/ xxx-xxxx

Best regards,

Rich Pisani
Talent Executive

Date:	Mon, 02 Jun 2003 14:18:50 -0700 (PDT)
From:	"Gabe Kaplan" <gabe@gabekaplan.com>
Subject:	To Rich Pisani about Star Dates
To:	stardates@eentertainment.com

Dear Rich,

Sorry it has taken me a while to answer. I've been thinking about my lifestyle and how to make it gel with Star Dates. Since you are under a tight deadline, I'll tell you what I'd like to do and you can decide whether or not it works. Would it be possible to have my two dates together and make it a threesome? If everybody likes everybody, nobody has to go home. Naturally, you'd have to find women who are prone to doing something like this.

Age and physical beauty are not important to me but I do like women that have a bounce in their step and a spunky attitude. No deep thinkers. I don't want to hear anything about current events or astrology. If they like hot tubs and Jose Cuervo, that's a good beginning.

Tell the gals that I'm a good cook and enjoy whipping up an old-fashioned country breakfast with all the trimmings. In fact, the whole crew is invited to join us.

Let me know what E! and Star Dates think about this proposal.

Gabe
gabe@gabekaplan.com

Date:	Mon, 02 Jun 2003 14:26:00 -0700
From:	"Rich Pisani" <stardates@eentertainment.com>
Subject:	FW: To Rich Pisani about Star Dates
To:	gabe@gabekaplan.com

Gabe, sounds very interesting. Let me run it by the producers and get back to you.

Date:	Wed, 04 Jun 2003 10:04:52 -0700
From:	"Rich Pisani" <stardates@eentertainment.com>
Subject:	Re: Star Dates
To:	gabe@gabekaplan.com

I'm sorry that I haven't gotten back to you.
It went up to "committee" and some really like
the idea and some felt we should stick to the
original format. I was waiting for everyone
to come to a unanimous consensus. I totally
understand you moving on and sorry for not
getting back to you. I too think they missed the
boat here.

Thank you for considering it.

Date:	Thu, 05 Dec 2002 14:16:52 -0800 (PST)
From:	"Gabe Kaplan" <gabe@gabekaplan.com>
Subject:	Ready For Sobriety
To:	webmscorrespondence@aaany.com

Dear Triple A,

Believe me it's taken a long time to finally write this letter. As you know, denial is a powerful emotion. We convince ourselves that we really don't have a problem because we think we can stop whenever we want. And the problem is especially magnified if you're a known person.

So I'm finally swallowing my pride and reaching out to your fine organization. I know that AAA has saved many a lost soul like myself. I didn't join previously because I thought it was a sign of weakness, but now I've seen the light. Could you please send me a list of locations in my area where you conduct your meetings?

Also, I've seen your stickers pasted on the bumpers of your members' cars. Please enclose one in my "welcome aboard" package. It's going right on my bumper because I'm not ashamed anymore.

I'm aware that if an AAA member slips up and gets in trouble while driving, you provide roadside assistance. I'd like to sign up for that service, too. (Better safe than sorry). That's about it for now. I'm on the road to sobriety.

Takin' it one day at a time,

Gabe Kaplan
gabe@gabekaplan.com

PS Just out of couriosity, before he quit, what was Bill W's favorite drink?

Date:	Fri, 06 Dec 2002 14:52:32 -0800
From:	"automotive" <automotive@aaaemail.com>
Subject:	Re: Automotive: Other [#97015]
To:	gabe@gabekaplan.com

Hello,

I think you are getting AAA mixed up with AA.
AAA does not provide an counseling and AA does
not provide towing. Please let me know if I can
answer anything else.

And by the way, I have no idea what Bill W's
favorite drink was.

Sincerely,
CSAA Support Team

Date: Tue, 20 May 2003 14:15:39 -0700 (PDT)
From: "Gabe Kaplan" <gabe@gabekaplan.com>
Subject: I never Metamucil I didn't like
To: cagarc@procgam.com

Dear Ms. Garcia,

As Will Rogers once said, "I never Metamucil I didn't like." I'd have to agree. For the past six years, I've been using your wonderful product. Regularly, you might say. My only complaint: it took me awhile to find out about your product. You don't have an effective advertising campaign. Take Wheaties, to sell their cereal to kids they put major sports stars on the box - Tiger Woods, Michael Jordan, etc. How about this idea to help sell *your* products to the proper demographic: pictures of constipated celebrities.

How would the public know who's constipated? You show before-and-after pictures of a noted celebrity. Before, stuffed up and uncomfortable. After, cleaned-out and ready to tackle the world. I've enclosed two pictures of myself to show how effective I believe this advertising ploy can be.

Where do we go after Kaplan, you might ask? The choice is endless. Believe me, I don't know one older celebrity who isn't constipated. Let's just say it's all we talk about at celebrity autograph shows. So let's get this campaign off the pot, Metamucil. No sense flushing away valuable time. Let's get this movement going. I'll stop myself at this point.

The ball's in your tank,

Gabe Kaplan
gabe@gabekaplan.com

270 N. Canon Dr.
Suite1404
Beverly Hills, CA 90210

PS Let's get some more new flavors.

before Metamucil

after Metamucil

Date:	Mon, 02 Jun 2003 14:17:30 -0400
From:	"Carmen Garcia" <cagarc@procgam.com>
Subject:	Re: Follow-up
To:	gabe@gabekaplan.com

Dear Mr. Kaplan,

I apologize for the delay in responding. I submitted your offer to the team but decisions about current adds have been made.

Thanks you for your interest in our products.

Sincerely,
Carmen S. Garcia, Ph.D
External Relations / Personal Health Care
Procter & Gamble

Date:	Fri, 07 Mar 2003 21:17:21 -0800 (PST)
From:	"Gabe Kaplan" <gabe@gabekaplan.com>
Subject:	A question about Stalin
To:	jgad@yale.edu

Dear Prof. Gaddis,

My name is Gabe Kaplan. If you're not familiar with me, I am a Russian-born American actor and history buff. For the last ten years, I've been free to pursue my hobby of researching life in Russia during the Stalin era. As an expert in 20th century Russian political history, I am hoping you can help me out.

There is one area of Stalin's character that is either largely unknown or purposely ignored by historians and biographers. Now that it's the fiftieth anniversary of his death, I feel it should come out (if, of course, it's true). Before I begin, let me tell you that I have personally confirmed this story by talking to one actual eyewitnesses, the offspring of actual eyewitnesses, and people who just heard it through the grapevine.

It seems Joseph Stalin was a practitioner of genital origami, the ancient art of manipulating one's genitals into familiar shapes and figures. Not only could he do the classic seven positions, he pushed way beyond that and took his passion to heights only achieved by 19th century Chinese masters. In 1946 he created his masterpiece when he twisted his package into a flock of geese migrating over the Kamchatka peninsula.

I have heard his remarkable gift was, at first, completely unappreciated by everyone in the Kremlin. However, with time, they actually looked forward to these performances and their applause and excitement was genuine. Even Beria became completely intrigued with the dicktator's hobby. Please let me know what knowledge you have of this curious aspect of Stalin's personality.

Let's share information,

Gabe Kaplan
gabe@gabekaplan.com

PS There is rumored to be a photograph of Stalin practicing his passion. Have you heard anything about this?

Date:	Wed, 26 Mar 2003 15:05:29 -0500
From:	"Daniel Radosh" <drash@radosh.org>
Subject:	Stalin's art
To:	gabe@gabekaplan.com

Dear Mr. Kaplan,

I'm a writer with Radar magazine in New York City. I've already left a message at what I gather was your home (I apologize for any intrusion; it was the only phone number I could find), but perhaps I can reach you more quickly this way.

I wanted to ask you about the e-mail concerning Stalin and genital origami that you recently sent to historian John Gaddis (you had to know it would be forwarded around!). Unfortunately I'm on a very tight deadline, but if you have a minute to talk, please give me a call.

Thanks,

Daniel

INTELLIGENCE

For his part, Peres, denies reports that the fey magazine is finally coming out. "I'll have **HEATHER GRAHAM'S** nipple in the magazine," Peres promises, "or **COLIN FARRELL** getting tons of ass—female ass!" *Riiight*. How then to explain a recent cover on which the magazine asked its readers, "Have you had sex with Colin Farrell yet?" Perhaps this is a question we should pose to *Details*' new sex columnist. Yep, he's gay.

▶ **CLUB KING PETER GATIEN JUST CAN'T CATCH A BREAK**
After years of police and Justice Department investigations, the former nightlife impresario and producer of *A Bronx Tale* was poised to return to his roots. According to Gatien, he and director **SPIKE LEE** had agreed to develop a weekly television series set in a trendy New York nightclub. The fictional series, tentatively titled *Limelight*, after Gatien's now padlocked clubs in London, Atlanta and New York, was to be a cross between "*Moulin Rouge* and *Cheers*," featuring "a black DJ, a gay guy, and an aspiring actress." (Which, come to think of it, sounds oddly like our fact-checking department.) Unfortunately for Gatien, his past caught up with him when his longtime nemesis, former *New York Post* columnist **JACK NEWFIELD**, secured a meeting with Lee, and threatened to "ruin him" if the show were ever produced. According to Gatien, Newfield produced a series of his own clips about Gatien misdeeds, which later proved to be inaccurate. Soon afterward, Lee's office called Gatien to say their deal was off. A positively miffed Gatien says he's disappointed that Lee didn't do the right thing, but he claims that plans for the show are continuing, thanks to interest from L.A.'s Endeavor agency.

▶ **WELCOME BACK, KOTTER**
The sitcom well may have run dry, but that's not stopping **GABE KAPLAN** from living his art. The erstwhile star of *Welcome Back, Kotter* has apparently become an armchair historian of the Soviet Union—and the Ivory Tower is abuzz over his findings. After research that allegedly included an eyewitness interview, on March 7 Kaplan dropped the following thesis to a noted historian at Yale University: "Joseph Stalin was a practi-

tioner of genital origami, the ancient art of manipulating one's genitals into familiar shapes and figures.... His remarkable gift was, at first, completely unappreciated by everyone in the Kremlin. However, with time, they actually looked forward to these performances and their applause and excitement was genuine." *Eeek*. Adding that "there is rumored to be a photograph" of the dictator's penile pursuits, Kaplan closed with a collegial, "Let's share information." Though the academic tells *Radar* he was wary of a hoax, he was clearly not one to sit on scholarly innovation. Noting that Kaplan's work "could add a whole new dimension to our understanding of the Stalin era," he forwarded the e-mail to a group of friends. From there it found its way to academics and writers, including **STEPHEN SCHWARTZ** and **CHRISTOPHER HITCHENS**. As with all mavericks, Kaplan has yet to be endorsed by the intelligentsia. But perhaps our Yalie is simply the only one not blinded by professional jealousy. We'll never know: Neither Mr. Kaplan nor Mr. Stalin could be reached for comment.

▶ **ALL IS VANITY; NOTHING IS FAIR** With the nation's attention focused on the war, **BARRY DILLER'S** attempt to freeze out fellow mogul (and longtime foe), oil man **MARVIN DAVIS**, went practically unnoticed. Diller—who recently ridiculed his rival's girth and compared him to a waiter—lobbied his good pal **GRAYDON CARTER** to keep Davis off the list for *Vanity Fair's* annual Oscar bash. The wing-haired power editor was said to be ready to comply until Davis threatened to upstage *VF* by throwing a star-studded party of his own on the same night. In these troubled times, the last thing we need is a divided A-list. The threat was convincing enough that *VF* delivered an invitation to Davis the next day. A magazine spokesperson denied this account but wouldn't offer another explanation. Both Diller and Davis declined comment. ᴿ

77

<table>
Date:	Sun, 01 Jun 2003 20:04:20 -0700 (PDT)
From:	"Gabe Kaplan" <gabe@gabekaplan.com>
Subject:	Fossil Hunters?
To:	drash@radosh.org
</table>

Daniel,

Thank you for following through on your promise and sending me the magazine I enjoyed it immensely. "You did the Mash, you did The Monster Mash". Of the sixty-five people you listed as monsters, I've had personal experience with about forty so I know whereof you speak.

By the by, I must confess that I'm a little miffed about my blurb in "fresh intelligence." You reached me for comment, and I did tell you it was a hoax. Because of the ambiguity, I have had two experts on communist Russia asking to see my "proof". When I told them the whole thing was a joke, they refused to believe me. It's just to wonderful to think of Stalin dropping his drawers and puppetting away. If anyone else calls, I'll refer them to you or Gaddis.

On another completely different subject, I don't suppose you have heard anything about the "Fossil Hunters"? Briefly, they are seven young women from Washington, Los Angeles and New York. All of them are trying to bed still-functioning icons of the twentieth century. It's a one year contest, the list is varied and the object is to do as many targets as possible.

It ends July 1st and I'm told it has produced some amazing results. They want a no-holds-barred account published when it's over. They will submit to a word limit, but no editing. Discussions have been under way with another publication, but the "no editing" thing is a big problem.

Let me know if Radar is interested. It would be the perfect place for this story. They want the article to lead to a film.

Gabe
gabe@gabekaplan.com

Date:	Mon, 02 Jun 2003 07:53:24 -0700 (PDT)
From:	"Daniel Radosh" <drash@radosh.org>
Subject:	Re: Fossil Hunters?
To:	gabe@gabekaplan.com

Hi. Glad you like Radar. Sorry for the confusion over the Fresh Intel item. We were on a really tight deadline, and it turned out that I reached you about a day too late to get your reaction into the story. Still, everyone got a kick out of it, which is the main thing.

The fossil hunters story sounds really great. Knowing your sense of humor, of course, I'd need to be convinced that it's true... But if so, it sounds perfect for Radar. I don't think we — or any magazine — would agree up front to "no editing," but we would certainly try to work out something that would satisfy the writers.

Keep me posted.

Daniel

Gabe Kaplan

270 N Canon Drive, Suite 1404
Beverly Hills, CA 90210
gabe@gabekaplan.com

May 3, 2003

United States Post Office
Washington, D. C.

Dear Postmaster General,

I know you're busy over there, so I'll get right to the point. Do you decide which celebrities get put on stamps? I'll tell you why I ask: I'd like to nominate myself for your next celebrity stamp. I realize a nominee must be deceased. But here's the beautiful thing, most people think I'm dead anyway. Think of it: what a hubbub this could cause, and what a collector's item this stamp would become once it was revealed I was, in fact, still alive. I would naturally pretend I was upset at the mistake in my life status, but at the same time act honored by my selection. Trust me, I can pull this off.

Being a general, you must know what it feels like to have a soldier you thought was lost in battle, and how wonderful the whole division felt when he mystically reappeared. It's always a big morale booster.

There are several photos of me that would be suitable for a stamp. There's the teacher in "Kotter," me in Montana, advocating for bighorn sheep in '86, or, finishing 12th at the World Senior Triathletes championships in 99

Can you discretely send me a list of what else I would have to do to qualify for this honor? I've never been arrested and I've only been sued once, plus I've voted in every presidential election since 1968.

Awaiting your stamp of approval,

Gabe Kaplan

PS I hate to bother you, but could you send me a "change of address" form.

UNITED STATES
POSTAL SERVICE

May 30, 2003

Mr. Gabe Kaplan
Apartment 1404
270 North Cannon Drive
Beverly Hills, CA 90210-5312

Dear Mr. Kaplan:

This is in response to your recent letter to the Citizens' Stamp Advisory Committee expressing support for the issuance of a commemorative stamp depicting a photograph of yourself.

Unfortunately, we cannot honor your request to issue a stamp with your image. Enclosed for your reference is the *Creating U.S. Postage Stamp* brochure which outlines the policies and guidelines for stamp consideration. Specifically, criterion number two is applicable to your request.

As information, each year the Postal Service receives thousands of letters suggesting hundreds of different topics for new stamps. The Citizens' Stamp Advisory Committee was established in 1957 to review all suggestions and make recommendations to the Postmaster General. Committee recommendations are based on national interest, historical perspective, and other criteria. We rely on the Committee to produce a balanced stamp program that touches on all aspects of our heritage.

Your interest in our stamp program is very much appreciated.

Sincerely,

Terrence W. McCaffrey
Manager
Stamp Development

Enclosure

16 WHO'S ON FIRST?

Date: Thu, 22 May 2003 11:08:37 -0700 (PDT)
From: "Gabe Kaplan" <gabe@gabekaplan.com>
Subject: Aunt Madalyne
To: bren@paho.org

Dear Ms. Brennan,

Today I had an interesting conversation with my Aunt Madalyne who lives in Costa Rica. It went something like this.

Her: Is everybody in California frightened?

Me: About what?

Her: The SARS disease.

Me: WHO says it's contained.

Her: No one. Half the people in China have it. It's not contained.

Me: WHO says it is!

Her: Nobody. Everybody's worried. Even here in Costa Rica. It's not contained.

Me: That's what I'm trying to tell you. WHO is The World Health Organization. They say it's contained.

Her: They are who?

Me: Right.

Her: What?

Me: The World Health Organization is WHO.

Her: Why are you asking me, you brought them up.

Me: They are the experts on communicable diseases. They follow outbreaks and transmissions all over the world. Nobody knows about these things better than them.

82

Her: Better than who?

Me: Right. Now you got it.

Her: I don't even know what I'm talking about.

Me: You know there's people that keep track of diseases.

Her: That's right.

Me: Did you know that they give reports to the press everyday.

Her: That's right.

Me: Those people. The ones that keep track of the diseases. The ones that give reports to the press. They're the ones that say it's contained.

Her: I don't know

Me: Third base.

I know your business is a serious one, but I thought you might get a kick out of this. You must come across some confusion in your press releases when you start them out with, "WHO says....."

Best regards,

Gabe Kaplan
gabe@gabekaplan.com

Date:	Thu, 22 May 2003 14:23:17 -0400
From:	"Brennan, Ms." <bren@paho.org>
Subject:	Re: Aunt Madalyne
To:	gabe@gabekaplan.com

Thanks. I needed that!

17 SHUTTLE BUDDIES

Date:	Wed, 22 Oct 2003 13:19:08 -0700 (PDT)
From:	"Gabe Kaplan" <gabe@gabekaplan.com>
Subject:	NASA Publicity Proposal...
To:	nlee@headquarters.nasa.gov

NASA Headquarters
Washington, D.C.

Dear Ms. Lee,

I called Ms. Ferguson today to propose the following project, however her voice mail said she was gone for the week and suggested I contact you. Here's my idea- perhaps you could be kind enough to forward this missive to the proper person at NASA.

When I was eleven years old I made a ridiculous yet earnest speech in front of my 5th grade science class. My thesis was that we shouldn't go into space without taking Martians with us. If we went alone, it would cause disharmony in the solar system. My absurd speech did produce one positive effect: the Wyzotski brothers who used to beat me up regularly now kept their distance.

Once I outgrew my childhood extraterrestrial fantasies, I became compulsive about following the real space program. From Alan Shephard's first ride in space to Gemini, Apollo and beyond, all the ups and the downs.

You can imagine my disappointment when the Russians became the first nation to allow a civilian to take a trip into space. Sure, the two men that went into space paid an enormous sum of money to do so, but still the Russians got the reputation of being good guys and not stuffed shirts.

I started thinking- how could we trump them? Supposing instead of one, we send three people into space together and not charge anybody a dime. Who are the good guys now? Here are the three people I had in mind: Jimmy Carter, Julius Erving, and myself. A politician, a renowned sports figure and a beloved entertainer. President Carter will go anywhere, and on this trip he won't even have to build anything. Dr. J and myself are both NASA fans and both of us happen to be available for an extended trip.

Talk about pizzazz! It would certainly cause a splash and not just on re-entry.

Houston, do we have a deal,

Gabe Kaplan
gabe@gabekaplan.com

PS Of course we would all pay our own transportation down to the Cape. (I know I will and I can't see the other guys not going along.)

Date:	Thu, 23 Oct 2003 09:38:26 -0400
From:	"Naeemah Lee" <nlee@headquarters.nasa.gov>
Subject:	Re: NASA Publicity Proposal...
To:	gabe@gabekaplan.com

I have received your request but I need more information, I provided a questionnaire for you to answer, as soon as I get this information I can start the review process. If you have any questions please give me a call or email.

Naeemah lee
Office Of Public Affairs

Those seeking the Agency's assistance with media productions must do so through a written proposal directed to the Manager of Multimedia, Bobbie Faye Ferguson of Headquarters, Public Affairs/ Public Services offices. Any proposal shall include the following information:

1. Identify who you are: name, address, and telephone numbers. Also include Producers and Directors who are working on the project.

2. Provide a short description of your project, where would it air etc.

3. Provide a script, treatment, storyboard or outline of the project in sufficient detail to allow the Agency to evaluate the project's objectives.

4. Identify the distribution or studio, network or outlet?

(Note - NASA does not collaborate on "spec." projects, i.e., a project that is merely a creative idea with no commitment from a production company or distributor.)

5. Are you willing to reimburse NASA for its assistance?

6. What type of NASA assistance is requested?

Date:	Fri, 24 Oct 2003 00:58:38 -0700 (PDT)
From:	"Gabe Kaplan" <gabe@gabekaplan.com>
Subject:	Re: NASA Publicity Proposal...
To:	nlee@headquarters.nasa.gov

Dear Ms. Lee,

Thank you for your prompt response. Here are the answers to your questions.

1: I'm Gabe Kaplan, and reside at 270 North Canon Drive, #1404, Beverly Hills, CA. 90210. Former President Jimmy Carter lives in Plains, Georgia and Dr. Julius Erving lives in Philadelphia. I don't have their exact addresses.

There would be no producers or directors working on the project, which means fewer opinions and less chairs.

2: In short, the three of us (Carter, J, and Kaplan) go up in space on a NASA mission. The project would be broadcast live via satellite all over the world. Movietone News will probably make it their only segment for the week.

3: There is no outline or script, because it's real life. I have attached a detailed storyboard (which I've drawn up myself), that should explain everything we're trying to achieve.

4: I don't have a commitment from either of the other gentlemen involved; I just know they're huge NASA fans. However, if one of them declined, we could get another noted American; perhaps NASA could be involved in the selection process.

5: When you say "reimburse", do you mean for ground transportation?

6: We will need three space suits, nutritional supplements, plus two window and one aisle seat.

Please let me know if I've answered all your questions satisfactorily. I hope you enjoy the storyboard.

Best regards,

Gabe Kaplan
gabe@gabekaplan.com

#5

NASA'S NEW CIVILIAN ASTRONAUTS RETURN TO EARTH

#6

UPON RETURN TO EARTH,
WORLD PRESS SALUTES
NEW ASTRONAUTS...

#7

...AND CHEERS NASA
FOR BEING THE
"GOOD GUYS"

...AND
SO, NASA
IS
HERALDED
BY THE
WORLD
COMMUNITY
AND VOTED
"BEST
SUPPORTING
SPACE
AGENCY!"

Dear Ms. Ferguson,

A couple of weeks ago, I e-mailed a concept and storyboard to your office. I'm just checking to make sure you received it. As I mentioned in the proposal, this project would provide great publicity for all involved. If for some reason you haven't received it, I'd be happy to re-send.

Best regards,
Gabe Kaplan
gabe@gabekaplan.com

Date:	Fri, 09 Jan 2004 02:19:59 +0000
From:	"Ferguson" <ferguson@nasa.gov>
Subject:	Re: Recent proposal...
To:	gabe@gabekaplan.com

Pleae contact me at the above email address if
you would like to meet to discuss the project. I
am in LA for the landing events at JPL for this
month.
Ferguson
NASA Public Affairs

Date:	Thu, 14 Nov 2002 16:02:41 -0800 (PST)
From:	"Gabe Kaplan" <gabe@gabekaplan.com>
Subject:	Name Change
To:	RCC@co.san-diego.ca.us

Dear Recorders Office,

For the last twenty years I have had problem after problem in my chosen profession. People would say I was "difficult" and "Napoleonic." Everything imaginable has been said about me, in fact, one producer even called me "coquettish." Fictitious and slanderous articles have been published in the tabloids. You would think they could find someone else to write about. My once glittering career has plunged into an abyss of finger-pointing and civil lawsuits.

To try and solve the mystery of my show biz demise I have squandered much of my paltry nest egg on psychics, herbalists, and closet organizers. I tried to contact Tony Robbins and Dr. Phil but neither would return my phone calls. On three occasions I've been on "hold" waiting to speak to Dr. Laura but never got through. My aunt, an old Beach Boys fan, even suggested I get in touch with Dr. Eugene Landy.

Yesterday I just happened to be watching one of my old television shows. Something started troubling me when they rolled the credits at the end of the episode but I couldn't put my finger on it . Then it hit me like an epiphany, my name is all wrong! Gabe Kaplan: ten letters, three of them "A's." What could be more of a career roadblock than that sorry moniker? How could it have taken me this long to determine the source of my woes?

I would like to immediately change my name to Raziel Eureka. Twelve letters and only two "A's." Please tell me how I can effect this change as expediently as possible. I don't have any time to waste.

Gabe Kaplan
gabe@gabekaplan.com
www.gabekaplan.com

Soon to be,
Raziel Eureka

PS "Raziel" is a boy's name, right?

Date:	Fri, 15 Nov 2002 09:20:37 -0800
From:	"Alice Brennan" <ARCC@co.san-diego.ca.us>
Subject:	Re: Name Change
To:	gabe@gabekaplan.com

Dear Mr. Kaplan:

In order to conduct a legal name change you must contact the Hall of Justice - Legal Name Change Section. The address is 330 W. Broadway, Rm 225, San Diego, CA 92101. I hope this information is helpful, and if I may be of further assistance please contact me.

Sincerely,
Alice Brennan
Sr. Clerk

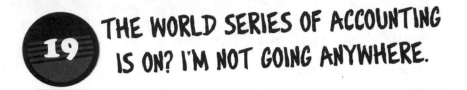

19

THE WORLD SERIES OF ACCOUNTING IS ON? I'M NOT GOING ANYWHERE.

Date: Sat, 22 Mar 2003 17:32:00 -0800 (PST)
From: "Gabe Kaplan" <gabe@gabekaplan.com>
Subject: Televised Accounting Event
To: bspaniel@calcpa.org

Dear Mr. Spaniel,

I've been a numbers guy all my life. My passions have always been budgets and investing. So I appreciate how you guys think. I'm also interested in cards. You may have seen me doing the color on the Poker Championship on ESPN.

It was so successful that the ESPN producer asked me if I had any other ideas for tournaments involving numbers and speed of calculation. I said, "what about getting the best CPA's together in one room and let them duke it out in the first ever World Series Of Accounting?" He flipped! He said, "five years ago, I would've told you, you're crazy, but in today's market it will work, if people will sit and watch twelve year olds spell for two hours, this will find its niche. It's great!"

Here's what I need : Exceptional accountants, with personality and a flair for the camera. If they're funny and have a fashion sense, those are plusses too.

The first year, we wouldn't mind localizing it to California just to see if the concept works. We would start out with ten competitors working on the same problem in an elimination tournament. For instance: A personal 1040 return, involving use of complicated tax codes would be given to each one. Then we would watch the fun break out as the numbers start to fly.

When it got down to two people, each of the finalists would choose (from a list of five) a problem their opponent would have to solve. Of course the studio audience, which would be made up of knowledgeable peers, would be screaming advice to the contestants as they made their decision. Then they square off as they try to win the big one for themselves and their respective firms. This might be the first time the public will have the thrill of seeing a room full of accountants in action.

Any feedback on the show and thoughts on finding the proper contestants would be greatly appreciated.

Best Regards,

Gabe Kaplan
gabe@gabekaplan.com

PS We would of course hold off on taping this until after April 15.

Date:	Mon, 24 Mar 2003 11:01:23 -0800
From:	"Bill Spaniel" <bspaniel@calcpa.org>
Subject:	Re: Televised Accounting Event
To:	gabe@gabekaplan.com

Dear Mr. Kaplan.

Thank you for contacting the California Society of CPAs regarding your idea for a televised accounting program. I enjoyed "Welcome Back, Kotter," and I'm sure your planned accounting program would be professionally produced and of high quality.

At this time the California Society of CPAs is unable to assist you with program development. Our membership desires that we stress professional ethics, thoroughness, integrity, seriousness, and similar qualities in our public relations efforts. These are the standards that the vast majority of CPAs follow. The nature of reality television is such that it seldom matches the image that we hope CPAs project.

We wish you well with your project. Certainly, when your accounting program is broadcast, we will be watching it.

Bill Spaniel
Public Relations Manager
CPAs: Committed to Excellence

Date: Thu, 17 Jul 2003 22:26:16 -0700 (PDT)
From: "Gabe Kaplan" <gabe@gabekaplan.com>
Subject: I'd Like To Sell My House, But . . .
To: gregg@coldbanker.com

Dear Gregg,

Last week I received a mailing you sent out. I'd like to run something by you to see if you think it is possible.

For a long time people have been telling me that if I sold my house I would get top value because of the fact that I, a major celebrity, have lived there for twenty years. Well I've fallen on some tough financial times due to the stock market and the fickle public's infatuation with lesser talents. I'm not bitter, but I have to be realistic about my situation. I was thinking of selling my house, but where would I move?

Then it hit me - if new homeowners would find it exciting to tell their friends that "Gabe Kaplan once lived here," wouldn't it be even more exciting for them to say, "Gabe Kaplan *still* lives here"? Here's my proposal: I sell my house at below market value but the buyer agrees to let me stay in the master bedroom. All I would need is one parking spot in the garage and I would take care of the complete maintenance of my bedroom, which has its own entrance.

Also, since my remaining family is on the East Coast, I would hope that the new owners would see fit to invite me to Thanksgiving dinners. This arrangement could work with the right family. I wouldn't even mind babysitting if the kids were well-behaved.

I'm motivated! Let's chat soon,

Gabe Kaplan
gabe@gabekaplan.com

PS The Thanksgiving thing is not a deal-breaker.

Date:	Fri, 18 Jul 2003 19:13:35 EST
From:	"Gregg Adler" <gregg@coldbanker.com>
Subject:	Staying in the house might work
To:	gabe@gabekaplan.com

Dear Gabe Kaplan,

First I want to thank you for responding to my
mailings. This idea is unique but it could work
with the right family. I have several ideas call
me direct at (805) XXX-XXXX. I am also curious
to know if you own any property in Calabasas.

Gregg

Date: Sat, 19 Jul 2003 20:09:05 -0700 (PDT)
From: "Gabe Kaplan" <gabe@gabekaplan.com>
Subject: Finding The Right Family
To: gregg@coldbanker.com

Dear Gregg:

I'm very happy that you think my idea could work. Believe it or not, I had doubts. There are a few Beverly Hills realtors that have been asking if I want to sell my house but I chose to write to you because I liked your picture. You also don't seem like a high-pressure guy.

If you don't mind, I would like to continue a short email correspondence before we talk personally. Can you give me a brief idea under what conditions you could see this kind of sale happening? Let's say, for argument's sake, my house is worth $2 million. What would be a fair amount to ask for if I wanted to still live there after I sold it?

Here's a possible scenario that I'd like your opinion on: The purchasing family agrees to try out our unique arrangement for a month. If everyone is not comfortable after that period, the deal is off and they just pay a month's rent.

This seems fair and very clean to me. However, problems could arise if they lived here for several years and then wanted to sell the house. Hopefully we will grow comfortable with each other and they will agree to take me with them to their next residence. Then they could sell my house and keep all the money, provided they'd always have an acceptable place for me and my bedroom furniture.

If I ever became incapacitated and couldn't care for myself, I could only be moved to a nursing home after Father Joseph DeMaria of Pomona agreed with the analysis of my condition. If he gives his approval and I'm unhappy after a month, naturally I could change nursing homes.

Let me know your reaction to all this, it's all a little confusing but it could work.

Gabe
gabe@gabekaplan.com

PS I don't own any property in Calabasas but I played golf there once and had a nice lunch at the country club. This is the only house I own.

Date: Tue, 26 Aug 2003 11:16:23 -0700 (PDT)
From: "Gabe Kaplan" <gabe@gabekaplan.com>
Subject: To Jim Kaiser: About GK And The Pips
To: theforum@mfx.net

Dear Jim Kaiser,

I have been looking for the perfect spot to debut an interesting new act. The Forum might be that perfect spot. We need a large reputable venue that occasionally features nostalgia performers and is somewhat under the main radar screen.

By combining the best elements of comedy, music, and soul group choreography; we are now ready to present Gabe Kaplan and The Pips. That's right, the original three Pips, including the legendary Bubba Knight, will be joining me in a mega-dimensional, multi-faceted, sensational new act.

We start out with me doing thirty minutes of rock 'em, sock 'em comedy backed up by The Pips performing in lockstep some moves we call "joke jivin'." Then, GK and the Pips do some of the famous signature numbers of the first GK and the Pips. Bubba and I alternate on lead vocals. By the time we get to "Neither One Of Us Can Be The First To Say Goodbye," I'm sure the audiences will be saying, "Gladys who?"

We close the show with a segment called "Pips-Squeak", where the Pips and I hold a Q&A period with the audience.

Remember, whether it's Gladys Knight and The Pips or Gabe Kaplan and The Pips the "GK" remains the same. We are in rehearsals now and should be ready to perform sometime after Thanksgiving. A rehearsal tape can be sent if you'd like to see it.

Sincerely,

Gabe Kaplan (GK2)
gabe@gabekaplan.com

PS Hope to hear from you through the grapevine. I have attached a photo. We should be taking new ones shortly.

Date:	Wed, 27 Aug 2003 08:34:50 -0400
From:	"The Forum" <theforum@mfx.net>
Subject:	Re: To Jim Kaiser: About GK And The Pips
To:	gabe@gabekaplan.com

Hello Mr. Kaplan,

Thank you for letting me know about your show.
Unfortunately, we become an ice arena from
October to March, then we are booked until
the middle of May. Perhaps we can look into
something for then. Thanks again,

Jim Kaiser
Forum Director

Dear Jim,

Thank you for your response. This is an amazing coincidence. There is an idea I've been kicking around for some time. I'd like to do a show called "Doo Wop On Ice". A few of the old Doo Wop artists are excellent skaters. This includes the Pips. Unfortunately I can't skate to save my life!

Here is my encapsulated proposal for

"Gabe Kaplan's 'Doo Wop On Ice'"

THE MARCELS MOON THEME

The Marcels (excellent skaters) open the show by singing "Blue Moon" then skate with women dressed as extraterrestrial "lunar ladies". They close their set with three or four of their other big hits.

THE CADILLACS GENERATIONAL ONE-ONEUPMANSHIP

The Cadillacs are on second and open with "Speedo". Then, after the vocal, as the upbeat "Speedo" music keeps playing, a group of younger skaters comes on the ice. We then have a generational one-oneupmanship where everybody does their best Hot Dog skating moves. Then the kids go to the microphone and sing some of today's songs while The Cadillacs shake their heads disapprovingly. The audience good-naturedly takes sides on which music they prefer.

INTERMISSION

JOHNNY MAESTRO & THE BROOKLYN BRIDGE
EAST RIVER THEME

On one side of the ice is a set resembling Brooklyn. On the other side, Manhattan. Each side has skaters dressed appropriately. The Brooklyn people are dressed as everyday common folk (butchers, bakers, candlestick-makers) and the Manhattan skaters are the "elite" (tuxedos and evening gowns). Johnny & The B.B. sing and skate with both sides, changing their wardrobe from "elite" to "common". The Marcels and The Cadillacs have agreed to do some of the character skating parts. Concluding this segment, the Brooklyn side and the Manhattan side come together on center ice and everybody joins Johnny to sing "That's The Worst That Can Happen"

THE PIPS: FROM GLADYS TO GABE

We close the show. The Pips sing and skate with a lady who resembles Gladys Knight. They do a couple of their hits, but not the mega-hits. Then, while they do "Neither One Of Us (Wants To Be The First To Say Goodbye)", they have an amicable separation and Gladys skates off the ice. A round platform is moved to the center of the ice. Kluge lights rotate and the new act, Gabe Kaplan & The Pips, is introduced. As the audience reeks in the moment, we do our new act. The comedy is cut to 15 minutes and we sing the three biggest GK & The Pips classics. Then we do the Pipsqueak question and answer session. I'm sure the first question to me will be "Why don't you skate?" Don't worry, I have a real funny answer for that one.

Are all your ice shows booked until the end of March? Ideally what I'm looking for is a week's booking and a week's rehearsal. I could start putting the show together immediately.

Best Wishes,

Gabe Kaplan
gabe@gabekaplan.com

Date:	Thu, 04 Sep 2003 08:37:26 -0400
From:	"The Forum" <theforum@mfx.net>
Subject:	Re: To Jim Kaiser
To:	gabe@gabekaplan.com

Hello,

The event sounds interesting but all our ice is already sold with the exception of late night. If we were to do this type of event I would have to start much earlier than this just to make the ice time available. One other thing, we don't promote in house. You would have to promote the event or we would have to come up with an outside promoter. Sorry I didn't get back to you right away. Let me know if this is something you are interested in.

Jim Kaiser
Forum Director

Date:	Tue, 09 Sep 2003 13:13:51 -0700 (PDT)
From:	"Gabe Kaplan" <gabe@gabekaplan.com>
Subject:	Time of late, late night and suit shining capabilities
To:	theforum@mfx.net

Jim,

When you say late night, what time are you talking about? Remember, all the doo-wop artists are members of the AARP. We might be able to sing late night but I don't know about the skating. When you let me know the time, I'll check it out with them. Also, we need to get our suits shined before every performance. Do you have a wardrobe person who handles that?

Best regards,

Gabe
gabe@gabekaplan.com

Date:	Wed, 10 Sep 2003 08:38:13 -0400
From:	"The Forum" <theforum@mfx.net>
Subject:	Re: Time of late, late night and suit shining capabilities
To:	gabe@gabekaplan.com

Gabe,

We do not have the capability of doing non-ice
events during hockey season unless we cancel ice
time so we could set up. Your event is something
we would have to look at later in the year.

22 HOW MUCH IS THAT SWEATHOG IN THE WINDOW?

Date:	Fri, 29 Nov 2002 11:25:13 -0800 (PST)
From:	"Gabe kaplan" <gabe@gabekaplan.com>
Subject:	Celebrity Auction
To:	darren.julien@entertainmentrarities.com

Dear Mr. Julien,

It seems that some of the biggest profit-generating auctions involve the sale of celebrity possessions and memorabilia. The Windsors, Jackie O, and, of course, Marilyn (Monroe). "Welcome Back Kotter," the show I created and starred in, has become part of the pop cultural zeitgeist. As a result, I feel baby boomers will pay practically anything to own a unique piece of the Kotter franchise. A single individual possesses the one-of-a-kind items most desired by well-heeled collectors of WBK merchandise, and you're looking at him.

I have in my vault, among other things, the Arnold Horshack lunchbox used on the pilot episode, all the actual letters from Epstein's mother, Mr. Woodman's truss and codpiece, worn on every episode and left to me in his will as a joke, Freddie Washington's Afro pick, which I even used on occasion, several rungs from the real Kotter fire escape, the maternity dress Mrs. Kotter wore on the way to the hospital to give birth, the twins' outfits, and, of course, the green Kotter jacket with patches on the elbows worn on the first show of every season. Here are some other items:

To the dismay of my fellow cast members, I had a habit of wearing the same clothes to the first day of rehearsal every week for four years. All of these items are in reasonably good shape- A Brooklyn College sweatshirt, OP corduroy shorts, Converse Sneakers, a pair of white tube-socks and size 32/34 briefs

The chalk and erasers that were used (sparingly) for the entire four years of the show

The apple that was on my desk in the pilot episode. I've preserved and mounted it in a baseball display case

During the times Marcia Strassman and I weren't talking, we communicated by hand-written notes, most of which include expletives

I've been bald since I was 24, and had to wear Afro wigs on the show. Three different ones of various lengths were used on "Kotter". Also, one year I did an electric razor commercial in Japan for which I had to shave my trademark mustache. Therefore, during the last four shows of the '77-'78 season, I wore a fake mustache. Two of the wigs and the moustache are in good shape. One of my dogs had his way with the other wig, and I don't know if it's sellable

The book "Beginning Scientology" given to me by John Travolta

Every year, the network gave out Christmas and birthday gifts to the stars of their shows. I have all eight of my presents, including the cards that accompanied them, signed by Michael Eisner, Marcy Carsey, Tom Werner and Fred Silverman. Most of the notes are the usual holiday fare, but some are quite interesting and saucy

 In fact, as an additional present one year, one of the above executives sent each of the male stars a plaster of Paris kit so we could make molds of our private parts for our wives or girlfriends. (It was Hollywood in the 70's). Naturally, my kit is still wrapped in its original box. I leave it to your discretion as to whether or not this is a saleable item

I also have mint Barbarino stuff. No telling how much it's worth. The aforementioned items would "get the folks in the tent," as they say, and there are many more unique objets d'arts to complete the inventory.

Going once,

Gabe Kaplan
gabe@gabekaplan.com

PS I almost sold all my stuff to one buyer because of the '86 market crash. I guess we're both happy, my sister loaned me some money and I didn't have to do it.

Date:	Tue, 17 Dec 2002 13:27:11 -0800
From:	"Darren Julien" <darren.julien@entertainmentrarities.com>
Subject:	Welcome Back Kotter Property on Sothebys.com
To:	gabe@gabekaplan.com

Hello Gabe,

Thank you for your email. This is a great list of items from an iconic show. I have listed below conservative reserves and estimates for your collection. Please do not be alarmed at my reserves and estimates for they are definitely low. It is best to start items low and let the bidding and market take them to their actual value. In many of our sales, we sell the items for more than the high estimate when we start low. Recently I had a second Seinfeld Sale and estimated the Puffy Shirt for $3,000 - $6,000 and it sold for $15,300. Most of the original scripts sold for more than $1,000. There are two things that we can do to insure that we maximize the value of your property: 1. Include photographs with each listing showing the item being used on the show. 2. Include a signed letter of authenticity from you (we will make these up, have you approve and sign). There are enough significant items in your collection that we could make a "Welcome Back Kotter" sub category all its own in our Hollywood Sale on Sothebys.com. We are building our next Hollywood Sale for March and we really like to include your items. I have attached a copy of our contract for your review. Once you have had a chance to look it over, please give me a call with any questions that you might have. After you are comfortable with the contract and would like to proceed, I can either make arrangements with you to pick up the property or have you deliver it to our offices. Thanks Gabe

for your consideration in working with us for I
appreciate the opportunity.

Best,

Darren Julien
President

1. The Arnold Horshack lunchboxes used
   throughout the run of the show - Reserve:
   $100 $250 - $500 (each)

2. All of the actual letters from Epstein's mother
   (12) - Reserve: $100 Estimate: $250 - $500
   (each)

3. Mr. Woodman's truss and codpiece, worn on
   every episode and left to me in his will as a
   joke - Reserve: $250 Estimate: $500 - $750

4. Freddie Washington's Afro pick, which I even
   used on occasion - $100 Estimate: $250 - $500

5. The green Kotter jacket with patches on the
   elbows worn on the first show of every season
   - $500 Estimate: $750 - $1,000

6. Several rungs from the real Kotter fire escape -
   Reserve: $100 Estimate: $200 - $400 (each)

7. The maternity dress Mrs. Kotter wore on the way to
   the hospital - Reserve: $250 Estimate: $500 - $750

8. To the dismay of my fellow cast members, I
   had a habit of wearing the same clothes to
   the first day of rehearsal every week for four
   years. All of these items are in reasonably
   good shape- A Brooklyn College sweatshirt, OP
   corduroy shorts, Converse Sneakers, a pair
   of white tube-socks and size 32/34 briefs -
   Reserve: $250 Estimate: $500 - $750

9. The chalk and erasers that were used
   (sparingly) for the entire four years of the
   show - Reserve: $100 Estimate: $250 - $500

10. The apple that was on my desk in the pilot

episode. I've preserved and mounted it in a
baseball display case - Reserve: $100 $250 - $500

11. During the times Marcia Strassman and I weren't
talking, we communicated by hand-written notes,
most of which include expletives - Reserve:
$100 Estimate: $250 - $500

12. I've been bald since I was 24, and had to wear
Afro wigs on the show. Three different ones of
various lengths were used on "Kotter". Also,
one year I did an electric razor commercial in
Japan for which I had to shave my trademark
mustache. Therefore, during the last four
shows of the '77-'78 season, I wore a fake
mustache. Two of the wigs and the moustache
are in good shape. One of my dogs had his way
with the other wig, and I don't know if it's
sellable - Reserve: $250 Estimate: $500 - $750

13. The book "Beginning Scientology" given to me
by John Travolta - Reserve: $250 Estimate:
$500 - $750

14. Every year, the network gave out Christmas and
birthday gifts to the stars of their shows. I
have all eight of my presents, including the
cards that accompanied them, signed by Michael
Eisner, Marcy Carsey, Tom Werner and Fred
Silverman. Most of the notes are the usual
holiday fare, but some are quite interesting
and saucy - Reserve: $100 Estimate: $200 - $400

15. In fact, as an additional present one year,
one of the above executives sent each of
the male stars a plaster of Paris kit so we
could make molds of our private parts for
our wives or girlfriends. (It was Hollywood
in the 70's). Naturally, my kit is still
wrapped in its original box. I leave it to
your discretion as to whether or not this is a
saleable item - Reserve: $100 Estimate: $250 -
$500 (If saleable).

Date:	Wed, 18 Dec 2002 10:16:10 -0800 (PST)
From:	"Gabe Kaplan" <gabe@gabekaplan.com>
Subject:	Kotter Items
To:	darren.julien@entertainmentrarities.com

Hello Julien,

Thank you for your prompt reply. Even though items can bring more than you project, I was disappointed with the reserves and estimated prices listed. I'm not questioning your expertise, just disappointed.

In most depictions of Mr. Kotter (games, puzzles, lunchboxes, trading cards) he is seen wearing the green jacket with the patches on the elbows. I had a vastly higher value in mind for that item in particular.

Mr. Woodman's codpiece was worn by a famous Irish actor and given to a young John Sylvester White as a show of affection and he wore it through most of his theatrical life. I also thought that would bring more at the hammer.

Speaking of hammers, if you ever watched the show, you'd know that Mr. Kotter was a klutz. He had a hammer, wrench and screwdriver that he was always unsuccessfully trying to fix things with (He was no Tim "The tool-man" Taylor). I still have all those items. The hammer was featured prominently on several episodes. On one, Julie hid it so she could call a handyman and not have to watch Gabe's ineptness. He had the Sweathogs and Mr. Woodman scouring the house for it. Any fan of the show remembers that episode. Anyway, I told you I had other items. That was one of them.

Let me think about whether or not I want to go forward, knowing your estimates were conservative but possibly accurate.

I'll contact you after the holidays.

Best,

Gabe Kaplan
gabe@gabekaplan.com

Date:	Thu, 19 Dec 2002 08:27:15 -0800
From:	"Darren Julien" <darren.julien@entertainmentrarities.com>
Subject:	Re: Kotter Items
To:	gabe@gabekaplan.com

Hello Gabe,

Thank you for your email! I completely understand and please do not be put off by the reserves and estimates. If you would like to only try four of five items in this first sale, you are more than welcome to do so. I think you will be surprised as to the results but we will definitely have to package them right (photograph of the items being used on the show and a certificate of authenticity signed by you). It is a pleasure working with you this far and I appreciate the opportunity to look at the list of some of your items. Please do not hesitate to call me on my cell phone if you have any questions in the next 10 days (818) XXX-XXXX.

Best,

Darren

Date:	Sat, 30 Aug 2003 10:09:49 -0700
From:	"Darren Julien" <darren@julienentertainment.com>
Subject:	Hello to you
To:	gabe@gabekaplan.com

Hello Gabe,

I hope you are well! I wanted to touch base with
you in regards to the "Welcome Back Kotter"
property. We have a large pop culture sale
in two weeks and I would like to mail you a
catalogue and invite you to the auction. The
sale will take place September 13th & 14th at
the Beverly Garland hotel in North Hollywood.
Please let me know your address and I will mail
you a color catalogue for the lots in the sale.
I will be having another sale similar to this
in a few months and would like to include your
property. As you will see by the results of this
sale, the estimates are low and most of the items
will tend to sell higher than the high estimate.
If you can make it to the sale, please make sure
you find me for I would like to meet you in person.
I look forward to hearing from you.

Best,

Darren Julien
President

Date:	Mon, 08 Sep 2003 2:45 PM
From:	"Gabe Kaplan" <gabe@gabekaplan.com>
Subject:	Re: Hello to you
To:	darren@julienentertainment.com

Darren,

Thanks for keeping in touch. Yes, definitely send me a brochure for Beverly Garland's auction. I remember when she married Fred McMurray on "My Three Sons". I suppose most of her items are associated with that show?

Is there a reason she wants the auction held in her hotel room? It all sounds a little strange to me but I guess everybody's looking for a gimmick. Are auctions like this effective?

With a theme in mind, what about if I had a auction garage sale? All of the items could be spread out across my yard, but it would be roped off and only invited guests could attend. This gimmick could stir up a lot of attention in the media. "Kotter to sell memorabilia on his lawn". I could even throw in some actual items from my garage to make it even funnier and more profitable.There's a lot of seventies stuff in there (tools, games and hula hoops). Also, how about a 92 Mercedes that only I have driven (90,000 miles, a couple of small dents but otherwise in pretty darn good shape).

Best regards,

Gabe
gabe@gabekaplan.com

PS: I make great lemonade and could give it out for free as an incentive.

Date:	Mon, 08 Sep 2003 14:59:25 -0700
From:	"Darren Julien" <darren@julienentertainment.com>
Subject:	Re: Hello to you
To:	gabe@gabekaplan.com

Hello Gabe,

It is so great to hear from you. I had to laugh
when I read your email for the auction is not
held in her hotel room but in her hotel. I
don't know about the auction garage sale idea
but anything is possible. You are more than
welcome to set up a lemonade stand at our
auction this next Saturday and I think that
you would do extremely well if you offered a
wide selection of Vodka to go with it. It might
encourage bidding as well. :)

Please email me your mailing address and I will
send out the catalogue right away. I hope you
can make it for I really look forward to meeting
you.

Best,

Darren

Date:	Thu, 14 Nov 2002 15:18:03 -0800 (PST)
From:	"Gabe Kaplan" <gabe@gabekaplan.com>
Subject:	Joining Mensa
To:	cloty@juno.com

Clotilde Cepeda
Testing Coordinator

Dear Clotilde Cepeda:
For a long time I have been thinking about joining your society. I'd like to know what the requirements would be for a noted person like myself. Let me tell you some of the things I'm capable of doing intellectually. There would be no reason for me to lie about these accomplishments because I would only be fooling myself. On an average day I can answer more than fifty percent of the questions on "Jeopardy." If you came over to my house you'd probably find me reading, or watching The History Channel. I know the capitals of all the states and could probably name at least 95 of the 100 senators currently serving. (I really never got into the House, there's just too many of them.) As for sports, I'm one of the few guys I know who understands how to compute a slugging percentage.

People are amazed by how much I know about all kinds of stuff. Unfortunately, I never did well on tests and didn't graduate from high school. So I realize I probably wouldn't pass your entrance exam. And that's a shame because I hear you do fun things like have dances and I would love to go to a dance and dance with bright people and talk about The History Channel and the economy.

If you want to take me out to dinner and ask me questions, go ahead. You'll be amazed at the length and breath of my knowledge. Remember what Mike Farrell did for Greenpeace.

Intellectually yours,

Gabe Kaplan
gabe@gabekaplan.com

PS I do all my own accounting and grocery shopping.

Date:	Fri, 15 Nov 2002 00:27:10 -0500
From:	"Clotilde A Cepeda" <cloty@juno.com>
Subject:	Re: Joining Mensa
To:	gabe@gabekaplan.com, AmericanMensa@mensa.org

Dear Mr. Kaplan,
Thank you for your message, and listing of your accomplishments.

Unfortunately, to join Mensa you have to pass our exam, or submit results of another IQ test you may have taken in the past. The fact that you did not graduate from High School does not mean you could not pass our test, as our test measures your intelligence, not your knowledge. Our membership includes other people who have never graduated from High School.

If you do decide to take our test, attached is the testing schedule, and instructions on how to register.

I am forwarding your letter to our National Office, in case they want to add something to what I have told you.

Sincerely,
Clotilde Cepeda

Date: Fri, 15 Nov 2002 11:43:00 -0800 (PST)
From: "Gabe Kaplan" <gabe@gabekaplan.com>
Subject: Too dense for Mensa
To: cloty@juno.com

Dear Ms. Cepeda,

Thank you for your prompt reply. It just goes to show that smart people are also courteous. At first, I didn't know what you meant by saying intelligence is different than knowledge. My 12-year-old daughter explained to me that knowledge is learned facts, and intelligence is how intelligent you are, and has nothing to do with learned facts. Einstein might never have answered Final Jeopardy correctly, unless, of course, the category was relativity or sweaters.

You must be a busy bright woman, so I won't waste anymore of your time. Last night I took your sample test off the Internet. Suffice to say, I didn't fare well. I couldn't tell which was the odd one out, between dogs and hamsters and rabbits. The number sequences drove me up the wall. I was perplexed if "Birds of a feather" was more like "Fine feathers," or "Two in the bush," or "One swallow a summer," and forget about completing any of those letter series'. However, if you want to talk World Series, I could tell you who won, every year, starting from the Black Sox scandal of 1917.

So I guess I'm too dense for Mensa, but perhaps you know of another organization where the people aren't super intelligent, but they know a lot of facts and statistics that they like to discuss with each other. That's probably the place for me.

Factually yours,

Gabe Kaplan
gabe@gabekaplan.com

PS Don't forget about the dances. I'd like an organization that has dances.

Date:	Fri, 15 Nov 2002 22:14:22 -0500
From:	"Clotilde A Cepeda" <cloty@juno.com>
Subject:	Re: Too dense for Mensa
To:	gabe@gabekaplan.com

Dear Mr. Kaplan,
I wish I could help you, but I don't know an
organization such as you mention. I'm sure there
is one, you just have to keep looking.

Best regards,
Clotilde Cepeda

IF I DID IT

Date: Fri, 15 Nov 2002 11:17:00 -0500
From: "Gabe Kaplan" <gabe@gabekaplan.com>
Subject: Steinmetz murder mystery
To: hlee@newhaven.edu

Dr. Lee,

We met a couple of years ago at the Connecticut Comedy Festival. I was the host and you acted as one of the judges. I made a joke about you saying, "I can't judge these people- they all alive!" You were laughing when I said that.

My parrot, Steinmetz, was brutally murdered yesterday. I couldn't sleep last night. Steinmetz was my buddy. I need closure. Would you come here and do a thorough forensic investigation of the crime scene? I collected evidence that the police refused to look at. Then again, the L.A.P.D. is notorious for botching pet homicides.

There are three primary suspects, all human. No cats involved. Steinmetz had a good heart, but he could insult people. In fact, he could be brutal. But that's no excuse to kill him, is it? Please come here and solve this mystery. I'll pay you and we'll get a lot of publicity if someone confesses. I won't touch anything until I get you're reply.

I'm not going to assume anything but if you like Chinese food, there are some great restaurants out here we can go to.

Sincerely,

Gabe Kaplan
gabe@gabekaplan.com

PS At the comedy festival, you had a picture taken of the two of us together. Could you bring a copy of that picture? I'd love to have it.

Date:	Mon, 02 Dec 2002 11:46:58 -0500
From:	"Henry Lee" <hlee@newhaven.edu>
Subject:	Re: Steinmetz Murder Mystery
To:	gabe@gabekaplan.com

Dear Gabe:

Thank you for your e-mail of November 15. I am sorry that I haven't responded sooner. I was lecturing in Bermuda and South America during most of November. This is my first opportunity to answer you.

Of course, I am so sorry to hear about the brutal death of your parrot. You must be very sad. Since it has been two weeks since you e-mailed me and you planned not to touch anything until I replied, I suggest you contact my colleague Dr. Michael Baden in New York City to review the crime scene. Dr. Baden is a forensic pathologist and he has a stronger stomach than I do.

Thank you for your kind offer to go out for Chinese Food. Perhaps we can get together the next time I am in Los Angeles.

I don't remember a picture of the two of us. I will look. My best to you and sweat hogs.

Regards,

Dr. Henry C. Lee

25 WHAT HAVE YOU DONE FOR ME LATELY?

Date:	Wed, 16 Jul 2003 13:18:31 -0400
From:	"Brand, David (HRSA)" <DBrand@hrsa.gov>
Subject:	Hello
To:	gabe@gabekaplan.com

Gabe (or Harold as we knew you back then), this
is to say hello to an old friend. I'm David Brand
from 332 Rogers Avenue, right around the corner
from 209 Sullivan Place, where you grew up in
Crown Heights. I just came across your E-Mail
address by searching your name in Google.com.

I have been following your career from the time
I found out that Kotter was you at a small re-
union from the neighborhood that took place on
Staten Island about 15 years ago. I used to
watch Kotter in the 70s (before I knew that you
were Kotter) and always had the feeling that
I knew the characters beyond their television
persona. Couldn't figure it out.

I have recently been in touch with several
neighborhood people from our time. The word is
out. They all knew about you.

Would love to hear back and start a conversation
with you. Please consider it.

Your old friend
David Brand

Date:	Wed, 23 Jul 2003 12:22:30 -0700 (PDT)
From:	"Gabe Kaplan" <gabe@gabekaplan.com>
Subject:	Rogers and Sullivan
To:	DBrand@hrsa.gov

Dear David:

It was great to get an unexpected email from you. Our paths haven't crossed for many, many moons. Last time I saw you we were two young boys waiting for life's adventures to begin. Well, how's it going? Have you gotten laid yet? Do you have your own drivers' license? Seriously, what really happened to you? Write me back and give me an encapsulated version of your last 45-50 years.

When you're writing back would you mind enclosing a check for $500? Even though I did quite well at one point in my life, lately I've fallen on hard times. I don't want to bore you with the details but I'm in need of a slight assistance. You're probably thinking that we really weren't that close. This may be true, but I always thought of you as an interesting guy that I wanted to know better.

You're in a more secure profession than show business and I'm hoping that this is an insignificant amount of money to you. Anyway, whether you send me this or not we had a great time back in the old neighborhood. Count your blessings that you've never been in drug rehab or had your face plastered on the cover of the National Enquirer. I know you're not the type of schmuck (like I was) that would've become involved in the militia movement. I chalk that whole episode up to misplaced patriotism.

See you on the corner of Rogers and Sullivan.

Gabe Kaplan
gabe@gabekaplan.com

PS Since you keep in touch with the old gang, let me know how they're all doing financially.

Date:	Thu, 31 Jul 2003 23:50:25 -0700 (PDT)
From:	"Gabe Kaplan" <gabe@gabekaplan.com>
Subject:	Any Chance for $250.
To:	DBrand@hrsa.gov

David:

Let's not lose touch again over a silly thing like money. I really would like to hear what paths your life has taken.

Perhaps it was a little gauche of me to hit you up for a loan after all this time. I just thought "Maybe my old friend is rolling in it." For all I know, you could be in worse shape than me.

If you don't believe this is really me, I can share several stories with you about the time I spent in your apartment.

Let me hear from you. We don't have another 45 years.

Gabe
gabe@gabekaplan.com

Date:	Mon, 04 Aug 2003 11:58:37 -0400
From:	"Brand, David (HRSA)" <DBrand@hrsa.gov>
Subject:	Re: Any Chance for $250.
To:	gabe@gabekaplan.com

```
Hello - Gabe. What is the relationship between
Gabe and Harold as your name? We knew you as
Harold. In fact, I had no idea that Kotter was
you because of the Gabe even though I got funny
vibes when I watched the show in the 70s.

Are you serious about the need for money? Tell
me what is going on. I believe that you are you,
but tell me what's going on.
```

I haven't seen you on the cover of the Inquirer, don't know what that is about.

What about the militia - don't know about that either? Drug rehab? What the hell is going on with you. Sounds like you have been pushing the envelope in your show business career.

Gabe - I really care about you, but tell me what is going on, please.

I am completing a thirty five year career in the United States Public Health Service, will retire next year.

I have been out of the office for your two messages getting married in Nicaragua —— really.

Write back soon.
David B.

Date:	2003 08:04:16 -0400
From:	"Brand, David (HRSA)" <DBrand@hrsa.gov>
Subject:	Re: Any Chance for $250.
To:	gabe@gabekaplan.com

Gabe - perhaps in my message yesterday, I did not make clear that I would be willing to help you financially; I just need more information about what is going on with you. Needless to say, I was a little shocked at your description of your current circumstances. I just assumed that successful show business people are permanently in good financial shape because of the amount of money one can make in that career. I also knew of the success that you had with

Kotter and that reruns are still coming over the airwaves and I assumed that you still received royalties from that. I also knew that I hadn't seen or heard much of you in terms of new stuff on the airwaves, that you had started once again doing stand up at Native American casinos (in Connecticut) and I knew NOTHING of the series of personal setbacks you described.

Your time in drug rehab concerns me. When did this take place? Are you currently remaining clean?

Gabe(Harold), I wrote to you because you were once my very close friend and I care(d) about you. I still do and would be willing to help.

Please write back soon with more detail. I am willing to help you.

Where are you currently living? The most recent address I have seen for you was some years ago in Van Nuys.

David B.

Date:	Fri, 15 Aug 2003 21:24:36 −700 (PDT)
From:	"Gabe Kaplan" <gabe@gabekaplan.com>
Subject:	Thanks for your offer
To:	DBrand@hrsa.gov

David:

Thanks for your generous offer to help, but it's not necessary now. I'll explain sometime in the future.

Gabe

IT'S A BIRD, IT'S A PLANE, IT'S ... AN ERASER

Date:	Tue, 07 Jan 2003 14:23:43 -0800 (PST)
From:	"Gabe Kaplan" <gabe@gabekaplan.com>
Subject:	Custom Eraser Plane
To:	p1aviation@hotmail.com

Dear Mr. Tjerina,

My business schedule has made it imperative that I purchase a private jet to fill my transportation needs. I would like to build a custom designed eight to ten seat plane.

Since the foundation of my success was built on the money I made by playing a teacher, I'd like the exterior of the plane to look as much like a blackboard eraser as possible.

I realize that any plane can be painted to look like an eraser, but that is really not what I'm looking for. Can you tell me if a plane can be altered into a rectangular shape and still retain its aerodynamics? If they can make the stealth bomber fly, why not a flying eraser?

I would be willing to sacrifice a little speed for an authentic eraser look. Would the cost be astronomical?

It's to bad I'm not John Madden and have five or six days to get where I'm going. I'm sure a bus could be made to look exactly like an eraser.

If this is at all feasible, the project could garner quite a bit of attention.

I do have my heart set on an eraser, but if you feel that's too ambitious, what about a Sharpie?

Best Wishes,

Gabe Kaplan
gabe@gabekaplan.com

PS Should my business expand, I may need a second plane. Then the two wouldn't have to be washed, they could just be clapped together.

Date:	Wed, 08 Jan 2003 22:53:15 +0000
From:	"Robert Tijerina" <p1aviation@hotmail.com>
Subject:	Re: Custom Eraser Plane
To:	gabe@gabekaplan.com

Gabe,

We can definitely get you a plane to seat 8 to 10 passengers and paint it like an eraser. As far as re-designing a plane to look like an eraser, it would be easier to have Saddam H. become an astronaut and fly to Mars with President Bush and John Maddan as his 2nd in command. It would be impossible and financially not feasible. It is definitely an interesting idea.

let me know if there is anything we can do for you.

Regards,

Robert Tijerina
Priority 1 Aviation, Inc.
Tel: 713-XXX-XXXX
Fax: 713-XXX-XXXX

Date: Tue, 14 Jan 2003 21:28:23 -0800 (PST)
From: "Gabe Kaplan" <gabe@gabekaplan.com>
Subject: Indian Caste System
To: darsh@dlshna.org

Divine Life Society

Dear Swami Sivananda,

In my life I have known several members of the Krishna movement. My best friend in high school, Sheldon Abromowitz, is still one. That's what drew me to your website. While you explain the reasons for the caste system in India, you also point out its injustices. I'm writing to you in hopes you can give me advice pertaining to the following situation.

For all of my fifty-three years I've been trying to find the right woman. Even though I was a major American television star I never ran across Ms. Right. Imagine my delight and excitement when I met Ms. Rahnee Gianjanpour last year on a trip to Liverpool. Though born in Bombay she's an ex-pat who is awaiting UK citizenship.

Last month we announced our betrothal. We are to be married next month at Leonard's of Liverpool. The guest list includes the Duchess of Kent, Deacon Jones, and Joey Bishop.

Two days ago I got an anonymous letter informing me that my intended was part of the "untouchable" class in India. My family is the Kaplans of Borough Park and we are members of the elite level of New York society.

My intended is an optometrist who has worked very hard to get to where she is. She is punctual, well groomed, and a delight to be around. Is there any way I can have her upgraded since she's marrying someone of my station? I'm not looking for her to become a Brahman, which I understand is the highest level, I just want you to kick her up a few notches so she would be acceptable to my family. Any advice given in this matter would be greatly appreciated by the American Guild of Variety Artists.

Caste away,

Gabe Kaplan

PS She may be "untouchable" but I can't keep my hands off her.

Date:	Thu, 16 Jan 2003 21:23:45 -0500
From:	"Darshini" <darsh@dlshna.org>
Subject:	Re: Indian Caste System (fwd)
To:	gabe@gabekaplan.com

Dear Gabe,

To 'kick your intended up a few notches' we suggest you contact the Borough Park Organization of Elite Optometrists. Suggest your 'intended' for membership, explaining that her qualifications include hard work, punctuality, and fine grooming. They will accept her and their acceptance will gain you some notches up the scale. If the B.P.O. gives you any problems, email the Duchess of Kent and Joey Bishop asking them to do what they can quickly for three reasons: to ensure a successful partnership between GK and RG, to assuage the Kaplan family, and to reassure the American Guild of Variety Artists.

Good luck!

Darshini

Date:	Fri, 17 Jan 2003 13:56:03 -0800 (PST)
From:	"Gabe Kaplan" <gabe@gabekaplan.com>
Subject:	Realizing Upgrade Not Important
To:	darsh@dlshna.org

Dear Darshini:

Thanks for your reply and advice.

For B.P.O., I found the Buffalo Philharmonic Orchestra. They said they knew nothing about the caste system or India in general, but said that Zuben Mehta did conduct there in the 70's. I don't think he was an untouchable, was he?

Then I called information, but there is no listing for the Borough Park Optometrist Organization. Are they located in Brooklyn?

At this point, I'm starting to feel, why bother with this whole upgrade business? We're going to get married, and if somebody doesn't like it, nuts to them!

If you're going to be in the Liverpool area June 14th, please be our guest at the nuptials.

Where is the Devine Life Society? Can Rahnee and I visit if we're in the area? Are you carrying on the teachings of Swami Sivananda? Did you ever meet Sheldon Abromowitz?

Thanks again,

Gabe
gabe@gabekaplan.com

PS If you come to the wedding, don't bring a present, we won't accept it. You've done enough already.

Date:	Sat, 18 Jan 2003 00:13:22 -0500
From:	"Darshini" <darsh@dlshna.org>
Subject:	Re: Realizing Upgrade Not Important
To:	gabe@gabekaplan.com

Dear Gabe,
We quite agree with your statement that if
somebody objects, nuts to them.

Thanks for the invite but it is doubtful that we
would find ourselves in Liverpool in June.
The Divine Life Society is global. Its founding
Headquarters is in the Himalayan foothills of
India. If and when you wish to visit our Ashram
in Rishikesh, India, let us know and we will
give you the email and fax numbers for the
General Secretary. You will need to write to him
for permission to stay at the Ashram.

Yes, we attempt to carry on the work of our
Founder, H.H. Sri Swami Sivananda Maharaj.
Sorry, we never heard of Sheldon Ambromowitz.

Best of luck,
Darshini

Date:	Thu, 19 Dec 2002 13:12:30 -0800 (PST)
From:	"Gabe Kaplan" <gabe@gabekaplan.com>
Subject:	Birding 'N' Hurting
To:	dporter@birdwatching.com

Dear Michael and Diane Porter:

As a bird watching couple, I thought you might be able to give me some advice on a personal problem I'm having with my own birding.

As I'm sure you know; it's very difficult to explain this hobby to folks who've never been bitten by the bird bug, which is my current problem. I am involved in a serious relationship and my new girlfriend, who I love to death, is a homebody and wants me at home, too. I've continually expressed my love for bird watching, but made it seem more like a casual hobby than the obsession it actually is.

Last Saturday night I had a performance in Galveston. I explained that since I hadn't made a sighting in over three weeks, I was going to stay over and try and spot the indigenous Black-Bellied Whistling Duck. She sulked a bit but there was no major scene. I said that this would be number 305 of a possible 689, but she couldn't have been less interested.

That Sunday in Galveston I got very lucky and spotted Mr. Whistling Duck within four hours. I immediately flew back, called her while on the plane, told of my sighting, and said I would be home in time for dinner. Although I knew she would not share my elation I expected some degree of enthusiasm, sincere or superficial. Imagine my surprise when, upon my return to our love nest, I found she had ordered a Peking duck dinner for two. She is half Chinese, but that's no excuse.

This was clearly a passive-aggressive disapproval of my extended time in Texas. I obviously passed on the meal, but did read my fortune cookie, which ironically said, "Don't lose sight of old friends."

I cannot give up my quest for the unsighted 384, but I also cannot give up my partner. I hate this bad time we're going through because in all other ways - sexually, emotionally, intellectually - she completes me and fills my needs. In your experience is this problem a common one? Are a lot of wives, husbands, or lovers completely unsympathetic to the sighting needs of their partners?

Any advice you can give would be greatly appreciated. Need my partner on my life list.
Best regards,

Gabe Kaplan
gabe@gabekaplan.com

PS Are there any support groups available?

Date:	Thu, 19 Dec 2002 15:35:45 -0600
From:	"Diane Porter" <dporter@birdwatching.com>
Subject:	Re: Birding 'N' Hurting
To:	gabe@gabekaplan.com

Hi Gabe-

This is a very funny letter.

If I believed you were serious, I would first
be surprised you had for even a day put up
with a person who so ill shared your interest
in birding, and who was so sulky about your
seeking fulfillment in this most agreeable and
meritorious activity. A person who has never
considered birds might be a fine person, but
if she still doesn't get it after a loving
partner has introduced her to the delights of
birding, then she seems most unsuitable as a
love partner. Birding would always be a bone of
contention between you. Better find someone else
and let her marry some boring fellow who will be
interested in something less earthy.

But then the story of the Peking Duck dinner
changed my mind. She sounds like a young lady of
humor or sympathy. I suspect she made you duck
to honor your success. Unless she knows you to
be a strict vegetarian, she must have thought
you an ungrate and a cad to refuse her offering.

And the fortune cookie! Now I know you've gone
mad. Why not read your destiny on the side of
the cereal box? Why would you take advice from a
fortune cookie, made up in some factory somewhere?

But then why would you ask for my advice, either?
Have I written anything on my website to make you
think I'm an expert in affairs of the heart?

I can't imagine why you sent me this most
entertaining letter, but I'm glad you did.
However, now I must return to writing an article
I have promised to finish this week. It's much
more difficult and less fun than answering you,
so I thank you for the diversion.

I would be glad to hear how your love affair
turns out. Congratulations on the duck. On both
of them.

Diane Porter

29

Date:	Mon, 02 Jun 2003 6:17PM
From:	"Gabe Kaplan" <gabe@gabekaplan.com>
Subject:	Classic Movies form - Charles Boyer
To:	ann@classicmov.com

Dear Ann,

Throughout my career, show business insiders have remarked on my uncanny likeness to the late great Charles Boyer. Our resemblance goes way beyond the physical. In 1973, I walked into a room where Marlene Dietrich stood some distance away. Squinting slightly she said, "eez dat you, Chawels?" Similar encounters have occurred throughout my adult life, especially the times when I've been clean-shaven.

I recently took advantage of this connection by writing a surreal one-man play. Clad in a tuxedo top and boxer shorts I recount all of Charles' life experiences while sitting in the bathroom. I call it simply, "Boyer on The Bidet." After five minutes the audience completely forgets the nature of the set and gets lost in the magic of this man's amazing life. People who have seen advance performances say it's like I become Boyer. The purpose of this unusual set is merely to say that Boyer is everyman and we are all Boyer. I feel I am doing my duty by presenting his life in this humble fashion.

As a Boyer fan and scholar I would cherish your input on this project. His second cousins, Cletus and Cloyd, saw it and were very moved. In fact, the Boyer brothers said it was a shame their late brother, Kenneth (who was the closest to Charles), didn't live to see the show.

Boyer lives,

Gabe Kaplan
gabe@gabekaplan.com

PS If you send me your email address, I can attach some pictures. You'll be amazed at the resemblance.

Date:	Mon, 02 Jun 2003 18:40:53-0400
From:	"Ann" <ann@classicmov.com>
Subject:	FW: Classic Movies form - Charles Boyer
To:	gabe@gabekaplan.com

Dear Gabe:

Thanks for visiting my site and for writing to me.
You play sounds "very interesting". Are you truly
the real "Gabe Kaplan" of Welcome back Kotter?

Sincerely,
Ann

Date:	Tue, 03 Jun 2003 11:19:32 -0700 (PDT)
From:	"Gabe Kaplan" <gabe@gabekaplan.com>
Subject:	Boyer on the Bidet
To:	ann@classicmov.com

Ann,

Yes, it's me. Thanks for replying so quickly.

Attached find a picture taken at the latest run-through. We've raised about 75% of the money needed to open the show. Since I speak French, (I spent two years in Belgium hosting Access Brussels) someone suggested opening the play in Paris. It's more on the line of French sensibilities anyway (even though they do spend less time in the bathroom) and people there remember Boyer. Most Americans seem to have forgotten. When the play opens here and they see me it should rekindle some fond memories.

What's your favorite C.B. film (after Gaslight of course)?

Gabe
gabe@gabekaplan.com

Date:	Wed, 04 Jun 2003 12:18:46 -0700 (PDT)
From:	"Gabe Kaplan" <gabe@gabekaplan.com>
Subject:	Hope you weren't offended
To:	ann@classicmov.com

Ann,

I hope my picture in the top hat, tails and boxer shorts didn't offend you. That's the play. I know it can be a shock to some people's sensibilities. Any relevant Boyer information you'd like to share?

Gabe
gabe@gabekaplan.com

Date:	Wed, 04 Jun 2003 19:04:51 -0400
From:	"Ann" <ann@classicmov.com>
Subject:	Re: Hope you weren't offended
To:	gabe@gabekaplan.com

Dear Gabe:

The photo did not offend me. Sorry, I just haven't had time to respond. However, I will be honest with you, I am having trouble deciding if you really are Gabe Kaplan. If it is the real "you", I apologize for my skepticism, but the web is a big place and there are lots of "crazy" people out there. Is there some other way you can identify yourself to me?

Thanks.

Ann

Date: Wed, 04 Jun 2003 20:32:07 -0700 (PDT)
From: "Gabe Kaplan" <gabe@gabekaplan.com>
Subject: Re: Hope you weren't offended
To: ann@classicmov.com

Dear Ann:

I can understand you being skeptical from just the post. But didn't you think that was me in the picture? If you're telling me that looked more like Boyer than Kaplan, I'm flattered. Why would anyone make up a story about a surrealistic play and then pose on stage for a picture like that just to get some CB insight? I'd have to be a guy that doesn't get out much.

Best,

Gabe
gabe@gabekaplan.com

Date:	Thu, 05 Jun 2003 09:31:17 -0400
From:	"Ann" <ann@classicmov.com>
Subject:	Re: Hope you weren't offended
To:	gabe@gabekaplan.com

Dear Gabe:

Believe it or not, it is possible for someone
to take your picture, edit it in PhotoShop,
place your head on another body that is sitting
on a bidet. It is also possible for anyone to
purchase your name as a domain, set up a web
site and copy your bio from the other site.
However, I think you have convinced me that it
is the "real" you. I hope you understand that
I'm not accustomed to having celebrities contact
me so, hence the skepticism.

I think its great that you are doing a show
about Boyer. We certainly need to keep his
memory alive and knowing your humor, its
probably really fun to watch. What made you
decide to use the "bidet"? Are you planning on
touring with the play? What else are you doing
these days?

Ann

Date:	Thu, 05 Jun 2003 23:43:03 -0700 (PDT)
From:	"Gabe Kaplan" <gabe@gabekaplan.com>
Subject:	Why Boyer
To:	ann@classicmov.com

Ann,

The main reason I picked Boyer in the beginning was the physical resemblance. However, the more I find out about him, the more I realize he is the perfect subject for this play. He is mankind. He is a guy's guy, but he has a feminine side. He is dignified, but has to use the bathroom. He speaks English, but with an accent. He is everyman. Plus he had a monogamous lifestyle.

Each century has an infrastructure. If you take apart the twentieth, you'll find Boyer sitting on top of the smoking pile, smoking a French cigarette.

Did I forget to tell you that I lived in Belgium for two years? I hosted "Access Brussels" so I'm fluent in French. We might open the play in Paris. So far, we have raised 70% of the money.

Gabe
gabe@gabekaplan.com

Date:	Mon, 10 Nov 2003 14:37:52 -0800 (PST)
From:	"Gabe Kaplan" <gabe@gabekaplan.com>
Subject:	Proposal for Gabe and The Boss . . .
To:	mlaverty@shfire.com

Dear Ms. Laverty,

As Bruce Springsteen's publicist, I'm curious to see what you think of the following proposal:

Bruce and I met back in 1975. I was in my first season with "Welcome Back Kotter" and he had a big hit with, "Born to Run." Good times, as the kids say. Bruce has continued to stay cutting-edge over the years with tours and new CDs. Congratulations to him! I've been really busy myself. Our careers, in fact, have run parallel since the beginning. He was on the cover of "Time" in October of '75 and I graced the cover some time in '76.

Which brings me to my point. Seeing as how we burst on the national scene together and since we continue to be pop icons, I thought it would be fun if we headed out on tour together. Maybe just a few dates at first to see if we draw, and then widen it up from there. The first night, I could open the show with 45 minutes of my family-oriented comedy and he could close it down with an hour of his best songs. Then the next night we could reverse the order. I've been doing a little research into the matter and it seems that late 70's nostalgia is huge right now. So a bill of "Gabe and The Boss" would definitely be very attractive to operators of the larger theaters on the circuit.

Anyway, please give Bruce my regards. And let me know what you think of the plan so I can put you in touch with my publicity people.

Let's go back to the Glory Days,

Gabe Kaplan
gabe@gabekaplan.com

Date:	Tue, 11 Nov 2003 08:22:26 -0500
From:	"Marilyn Laverty" <mlaverty@shfire.com>
Subject:	Re: Proposal for Gabe and The Boss . . .
To:	gabe@gabekaplan.com

Gabe, this is interesting, but it's hard to imagine Bruce doing it. I don't book his personal appearances in any event, so if you'd like to pursue this, please contact Bruce's booking agent.

Date:	Mon, 25 Nov 2002 15:06:08 -0800 (PST)
From:	"Gabe Kaplan" <gabe@gabekaplan.com>
Subject:	Career Advice
To:	tjones@careerplanningu.com

Dear Tom (TJ) Jones,

My show biz career started at age 19 and I've never done anything else since. Unfortunately, the amount of income I generate has dwindled consistently from its height in the 70s to next to nothing the last few years. So the time has come for me to face the fact that I no longer have a viable career in the entertainment industry. At 47 years of age I'm anxious to explore the different opportunities that would be available to someone of my background.

First of all, to be up front about it, even though I played a teacher on TV, I quit school at 16, so forget about any academic occupation or anything that has to do with math. I'm not really well coordinated and actually never even learned to drive. I have many allergies which means I could never work outdoors and I'm claustrophobic so I have to be in an open space indoors. Also, I have to wash my hands quite frequently.

Well, now you know all the bad things. Here's the good stuff. Most people still know who I am. I'm always ready with a smile and a pat on the back for anybody in need. I'm always prompt and well groomed with a nice smell about my person. And most important of all I'm willing to learn and do not expect success to come overnight. As a boy I built model airplanes so I would consider a job in an airplane hangar.

Please advise me about what our next step should be.

Looking to punch in,

Gabe Kaplan
gabe@gabekaplan.com

PS Is there any demand for a social director in an airport hanger, someone who told funny stories, organized activities and generally kept company moral at a high level?

Date:	Tue, 26 Nov 2002 08:13:22 -0600
From:	"Tom (TJ) Jones" <tjones@careerplanningu.com>
Subject:	Re: Career Advice
To:	gabe@gabekaplan.com

Hi Gabe. Great to hear from you. I replied yesterday to your email, but it was returned for some reason. So I'm trying again. I'd like to speak to you personally about your challenges. There are some realities to your situation that won't change.... therefore you have to work with your head, heart and soul to develop a plan to get you back on a new career plan and "back on top". I've got some ideas I'd love to share with you.

I'll be in my office on Wednesday, so you can call me OR if you want to set a time and date, I'd be happy to call you. I'm looking forward to our discussion. We need to talk....

Tom (TJ) Jones, PCCC, CPT
Author and National Speaker and Professional Certified Career Coach
Director/Founder Career Planning University

DISCOVER YOUR CAREER PASSION
http://www.careerplanningu.com

Contact information:
www.thetomjonesshow.com

Date:	Tue, 26 Nov 2002 11:45:15 -0800 (PST)
From:	"Gabe Kaplan" <gabe@gabekaplan.com>
Subject:	Career Advice follow-up
To:	tjones@careerplanningu.com

Hi TJ.

Thanks for you reply. Too bad you're not in the office today. Tomorrow I'm going to Laguna Beach for a second interview at the Ritz Carlton Hotel. They have offered me the position this summer of C.I.T. or Concierge In Training. It's indoors, in a large open space, I get to deal with the public and I believe the fact that I smell nice will be a big asset.

It won't start till June 15th, and if I do well, they'll keep me on as a full-time concierge in the fall. In the interim, the pastry chef can teach me to be a muffin man. I've never baked anything, but I'm told it's simple. I think they're going to politely tell me tomorrow that I have to do the muffin man to get a chance at the C.I.T. position. I'm a bit undecided and could use some direction.

Since Thursday is Thanksgiving, you probably won't be able to speak to me till Monday. Is it possible for you to email and briefly suggest what you think someone of my capacity and experience could hope for? I'll delay them till then. That would give me the weekend to digest your thoughts before we talk.

Looking for the right new leaf,

Gabe Kaplan
gabe@gabekaplan.com

PS Have you ever placed or trained a muffin man who wasn't already a baker?

Date:	Tue, 26 Nov 2002 16:54:50 -0600
From:	"Tom (TJ) Jones" <tjones@careerplanningu.com>
Subject:	Re: Career Advice follow-up 2
To:	gabe@gabekaplan.com

Gabe, just for clarification.... yes, I'm a
certified career coach and people pay me to
help them find their ideal career. But to be
honest, you are a "special case". Don't take
that wrong, but it's true. You'll have to admit,
you are a "bit unusual", and I say that in a
"funny and exciting" way. I have some ideas,
but it wouldn't be fair to share them until I
understand a bit more about you. After all, it's
YOU we are talking about and I'm not a "fortune
teller". Let's first build some trust and I
promise I won't try to sell you anything on the
phone.

Here's my promise to you. I won't sell you
anything on the phone. We'll only talk. I
need to understand a little more about you.
Would you be willing to complete a "profile
intake form"? It will probably take you about
20 minutes to complete. If you are willing to
complete that and have a "coaching" session by
phone (complementary - no charge), I can better
understand your situation.

Certainly, being a "muffin man" may be perfect
for you. But to be honest, I'll bet you that
that will only be a temporary fix. YOU must find
out what your idea career is, not just taking
something that seems convenient. People in
situations like you are so excited about getting
something, they jump too fast. And again, it
might be perfect for you, but let's talk first.
Again, no charge to talk.

And I won't try to sell you anything. If you are willing to meet me half way by completing the profile intake form, I'll email it to you. After I get it, let's talk. And yes, I have some ideas.... but I don't want to say what they are until I talk to you. I could be way off base and it would not be ethical to just throw things out without talking. Please feel safe.... I won't try to sell you on anything on the phone. PROMISE!!!

Tom (TJ) Jones, PCCC, CPT
Author and National Speaker and Professional Certified Career Coach
Director/Founder Career Planning University

DISCOVER YOUR CAREER PASSION
http://www.careerplanningu.com

Contact information:
www.thetomjonesshow.com

Date:	Tue, 26 Nov 2002 16:58:20 -0800 (PST)
From:	"Gabe Kaplan" <gabe@gabekaplan.com>
Subject:	Career Advice follow-up 3
To:	tjones@careerplanningu.com

TJ, Email the application, I'll fill it out, and we'll go from there. I'm a little excited about my Muffin Man C.I.T. interview tomorrow. I can sense you're negativity about this. You're the expert so I'll proceed with caution.

Gabe

PS Would you like any muffins if they give me some samples?

Date:	Tue, 26 Nov 2002 19:18:13 -0600
From:	"Tom (TJ) Jones" <tjones@careerplanningu.com>
Subject:	Re: Career Advice follow-up 3
To:	gabe@gabekaplan.com

OK, here we go. I'm attaching the Profile Intake Form. It's in Word format. Hope you can open it. It's no problem if you have Microsoft Word on your PC.

Answer the questions "honestly". Don't try to be funny. You must start with your real issues and your real answers. Don't take it wrong. I love comedy. But we have to start with a basis of factual information.

When you are finished, save it on your hard drive and then email it as an attachment. When you email it back, pick a time (remember I'm on Central) so tell me whether the time you'll call is my time or your time on Friday or Saturday.

This is going to be fun. Hang in there. Relax and enjoy the process.

Tom (TJ) Jones, PCCC, CPT
Author and National Speaker and Professional Certified Career Coach
Director/Founder Career Planning University

DISCOVER YOUR CAREER PASSION
http://www.careerplanningu.com

Contact information:
www.thetomjonesshow.com

Date:	Mon, 02 Dec 2002 11:15:33 -0800 (PST)
From:	"Gabe Kaplan" <gabe@gabekaplan.com>
Subject:	Actual Muffin Experience
To:	tjones@careerplanningu.com

Hi Tom,

Sorry I haven't returned your questionnaire. You should have it in the next day or so. Not to make excuses, but I had a very stressful, but enlightening weekend.

When I got to the Ritz Carlton, they asked me if I could work the Thanksgiving weekend, as the regular Muffin Man had the flu and couldn't leave his house on Drury Lane. They said it would be "On-the-job training." I told them I had plans, but they insisted and offered me time-and-a-half for the whole period. Some woman named Amy from the general manager's office seemed to be in charge. She said Thanksgiving at the Ritz would never be the same without fresh muffins and I should think about all the families and children that would be disappointed.

Then right after I started, she had the nerve to bring me out in my apron in front of the entire dining room and introduce me as their "Special Thanksgiving Muffin Man." I got a big applause, but so what?

Well, after four days of batter, berries, hot tins and ovens; I never want to see another muffin in my life. I'm surprised muffin people don't go postal. Talk about a monotonous, boring job!

Then before I left, that Amy said the general manager might consider putting a little picture of me on their brochure if I signed an agreement to be the Muffin Man for at least one year. I told her I'd think about it.

Best wishes,
Gabe Kaplan
gabe@gabekaplan.com

PS Plus, I gained two pounds.

Date:	Mon, 02 Dec 2002 19:50:42 -0600
From:	"Tom (TJ) Jones" <tjones@careerplanningu.com>
Subject:	Re: Actual Muffin Experience
To:	gabe@gabekaplan.com

You knock me out...... I have been laughing my head off reading your email. Don't want to say "I told you so", but being the "muffin man" just didn't sound right for someone of your status. And you do have status. It's just planning you career to take advantage of that asset. And I can help you do it.

I'll be looking forward to your profile questionnaire in the next day or two. Don't put it off. Take 20 minutes out of your "muffin" day and complete it. Don't agonize over it either. Usually, the first thoughts to questions.... are the right thoughts.

Tom (TJ) Jones, PCCC, CPT
Author and National Speaker and Professional Certificd Career Coach
Director/Founder Career Planning University

DISCOVER YOUR CAREER PASSION
http://www.careerplanningu.com

Contact information:
www.thetomjonesshow.com

Dear Tom:

Attached is my completed questionnaire. I answered the questions as best I could.

Let me know what you think,

Gabe
gabe@gabekaplan.com

Career Planning University

Helping People........
Enhancing Careers

Client Profile Questionnaire

Name: Gabe Kaplan

Address: 270 N. Canon Dr. #1404 Beverly Hills, CA 90210

Email address: gabe@gabekaplan.com

Marital Status: Married Divorced Single Widowed ***Other***

Spouses name: Carla and Rosie

Children's names: Davayah

Web site (if any): www.gabekaplan.com

Employer providing outplacement services: none

Your Position/Title: unemployed

How Long? Twenty five years

Your responsibilities at work: no job - no responsibilities

Describe how you liked your last/current job. Did you love it or hate it or something in between?

It was fun, I was making a lot of money and everybody knew who I was. Its was creatively rewarding and I got to meet John Travolta

Do you have a current resume? No

Educational background

Degree/ Certification	College/ University	Major	Year Obtained
Yes	PS 161		1957
No	Erasmus Hall High	Dropping Out	Considering earning on-line GED this year

What is your past experiences working with career coaches or consultants?

I have always taken consulting very well and been a team player. In the past, I've worked with wardrobe consultants. The results was that I always looked well groomed.

Have you worked with any career coach or counselor firm in the past? If so, who and when and what was the results:

The only counselors I worked with were at Ke Wee Ki, a summer camp I attended as an adolescent. The results was mixed. Some of the counselors were helpful, but one, Geoffrey, stole my favorite sweater.

Have you worked with a recruiting company in the past? If so, who and when and what was the results:

Marine recruiter in 1961. The results was, I failed the physical exam, but was encouraged to try again the next year.

Have you ever taken any assessments in the past? If so, what were they, when did you take them and what was the results?

My house has been assessed quite frequently, but I have not been assessed personally.

Have you ever been laid-off or involuntary displaced in the past? If so, who, when and what was the results?

The last year of my Television show, there were contractual disputes. Della Reese came in and played the teacher for a while. The results was bad for me and the show. Della Reese's results were much better.

Have you ever developed a systematic job search on your own? If so, when and what was the results?

I've systematically read the want ads in the paper for two straight months. The results was I've been offered a job as C.I.T. (Concierge In Training) provided I temp as the muffin man for six months, I'm going to reject that offer because of a miserable Thanksgiving muffin experience.

Write a brief story of your personal feelings and attitudes regarding your current career situation.

When I was on top, I thought it would never end. When it did, I kept telling myself, it was only a temporary. After twenty years, I'm starting to feel this is not temporary, and I better seek other employment.

What are your career goals and what career aspirations do you have right at this moment?

I'd like to find a good job that I enjoy doing and have nice people to work with.

Without disclosing personal financial information, how are you financially?

I've been better. I have enough money to last me the rest of my life as long as I don't buy too much. I'd still like to work though.

Have you received a severance package? If so, can you meet your immediate financial obligations and for how many weeks or months are you secure?

I don't believe I got a severance package when I left ABC. My financial obligations are minimal. I own my house and never eat in restaurants. I pay a lady once a week to come here and wash my dog. I will be getting a union pension and social security at age 62.

If you did not receive a severance package, how long can you meet your financial obligations (weeks or months)?

Thirty-six hours (just kidding). I'm just looking for something interesting to do.

NOTE: Our relationship is confidential. Unless you disclose issues, which is required to disclose to the authorities (e.g., intent to harm yourself or others), all of the content of our conversations will be held in confidence.

Is this confidentiality policy acceptable to you? Y/N Yes

How would you rank your current level of satisfaction with each of the following areas of your life?

Life Area	Very Satisfied	Satisfied	Dissatisfied
Work			
Emotional health		X	
Physical health/well-being		X	
Mental health		X	
Finances		X	
Spirituality/religion		X	
Relationship with spouse/ significant other		X	
Relationship with children		X	
Relationships with boss or coworkers	NONE	NONE	NONE
Social network/friendships		X	
Self-confidence/self-esteem		X	

What is your greatest success over the last year?

I picked up an old Rubik's Cube that I haven't played with in ten years and solved it in less than an hour.

What was your greatest success in your lifetime?

I won a football-handicapping contest in 1987. There were 43 entrants and I came in first.

What is your biggest challenge right now? Or asked another way, what factor(s) is/are holding you back from having everything you want?

My biggest challenge is organizing my clothes and sundry items in a way that provides for maximum efficiency. It should take me much less time to get dressed and polished everyday. That way I'd have more time to pursue a meaningful career.

Describe below your ideal life, assuming you could create your life exactly as you want it to be:

I would like to start off each day with a nice nutritious breakfast, then go to work at a job that's rewarding and challenging. Then, have a light lunch and go back to my job. I would like to still have enough time and energy to go line dancing twice a week.

What are your most important goals for the next 6 months?

My goals for the next 6 months are numerous and lofty. Get a good job, start writing my memoirs, participate in both a triathlon and a pie-eating contest (I've not done either), buy a disaster survival kit, fix my porch light and finally, keep one of the two women I'm involved with as a lover and turn the other into a friend or advisor.

What are you like when you are at your best?

Charming, compassionate, panoramic, with a zest for life and a love of people. When I'm at my best I don't leave any ten pins standing. I make all my spares.

Write a brief story about how you feel today. Write about where you are starting on this journey to find your ideal career.

Today, I'm feeling a bit under the weather. When I start my journey I'll be like Marco Polo, seeking new careers and undiscovered occupational frontiers that await me. You could be to me like Sacagawea was to him.

What else would you like us to know about you and your current life situation?

I belong to a group called Frontier Fathers. We believe in having our children mix with the offspring of the land. We believe that plants, flowers and people are all life forms and that a new understanding must start with the young. We meet once a month to talk and have snacks and drinks (all natural).

Date:	Wed, 04 Dec 2002 16:34:47 -0600
From:	"Tom (TJ) Jones" <tjones@careerplanningu.com>
Subject:	Re: Completed Questionnaire
To:	gabe@gabekaplan.com

Got the questionnaire. Thanks. Give me a couple days to review the answers and let's find a hour next week that you'd be able to call to discuss it. Again.... no money will be discussed. Just want to get a better sense of your needs after we talk and I've had a chance to examine your feedback.

I'm available Tuesday or Wednesday next week. Just give me a couple times that you are available so I can confirm them and block the time so we aren't interrupted.

Thanks for taking the first step. It's always the hardest.

Tom (TJ) Jones, PCCC, CPT
Author and National Speaker and Professional Certified Career Coach
Director/Founder Career Planning University
DISCOVER YOUR CAREER PASSION
http://www.careerplanningu.com

Contact information:
www.thetomjonesshow.com

Date:	Wed, 11 Dec 2002 14:01:42 -0800 (PST)
From:	"Gabe Kaplan" <gabe@gabekaplan.com>
Subject:	Where is Tom?
To:	tjones@careerplanningu.com

Tom,

I've not heard back from you.

Based on my questionnaire, do you think you will be able to find something rewarding?

Let me know.

Gabe
gabe@gabekaplan.com

PS I don't know if you want it, but here is the secret recipe for their famous Pear Nutty Pineapple Muffins

* 2 cups flour
* 2 teaspoons baking powder
* 1 teaspoon baking soda
* 1 teaspoon salt
* 1/2 teaspoon cinnamon
* 1/2 teaspoon nutmeg
* 1 pear, grated
* 1 cup oil
* 1 cup sugar
* 2 eggs
* 1/4 cup crushed pineapple
* 1/4 cup chopped nuts

Preheat the oven to 350 degrees. Sift together the dry ingredients. Place the, pear, oil, and sugar in a bowl and mix with an electric mixer until well blended. Add the eggs one at a time. Gradually add the dry mixture. Add the nuts and pineapple. Spoon into a wax paper-lined 12-unit muffin pan and bake for 30-35 minutes.

Date:	Sun, 29 Dec 2002 13:07:10 -0600
From:	"Tom (TJ) Jones" <tjones@careerplanningu.com>
Subject:	Where is Tom?
To:	gabe@gabekaplan.com

I apologize for the delay in getting back to you. The holidays and my coaching and development of a new speaking program has consumed me. BUT I WANTED YOU TO KNOW I STILL WANT TO WORK WITH YOU. Regarding your questionnaire, I'm very optimistic about your career future. I don't give out advice casually. As a matter of fact, a coaching exchange is not me telling you what you should be doing.... but rather, me helping you through a process on what YOU want to do with your career life. It will be amazing how you'll find it with my help. And I can almost bet I know what it is.

In today's wild and changing work world, there are so many opportunities for you, I can't begin to list them. Yes, I have an idea on what and where you should be based on the exchanges we've had by email and through your questionnaire, but it would be unethical for me to give them to you without an agreement. <u>I really don't know what you are fearful of concerning a telephone conversation.</u> At first, you said you didn't want to talk to me because you were afraid I'd sell you something. I tried to alleviate that concern by saying I'd not discuss anything about money during our first FREE consultation. Yet, you are still fearful to talk about it.

Gabe, I can help you. I can help you discover your career passion and help you find that ideal career that will not only turn you on to a new level of excitement, but I can help you learn how to do it so it "helps" people and you will leave a legacy behind that is greater than the Kotter period of your life.

Some time you have to trust someone. I'm trying to build a bit of trust with you so you can open up and we can begin to take a journey that will give you complete and total satisfaction and happiness you didn't think possible. Yes, we can do it together.

You took a major step by responding to the questionnaire. There is some wonderful nuggets of hope in there and I want to help you turn those nuggets into a success you will love. Please, give me a chance to help you. I want you to be able to say some day, "TJ helped". That's my goal. That's my desire. What is yours?

If you want, I'll call you. Usually my clients call me, but if it's the expense, I'll call you. I'm making you my special project this year. Let's work together.

I'll close with this one thought. I know exactly where you should be. AND I bet when we finish, YOU'LL discover it on your own through a process of coaching. Don't let "chance" impede your happiness and success in a career. Remember, you went out on your own to be the "muffin man" and that didn't work out too well did it. So why not let a professional work with you to remove that "chance" thing so you'll have purpose and value to your career life. Again, the first conversation is simply to get to know each other on a personal basis so we can move forward. After we have the first one-on-one phone conversation, you can decide what you want to do next. It's YOU that is important, not ME. Let's break that "fear" thing that impedes your progress. Let's talk.

Tom (TJ) Jones, PCCC, CPT
Author and National Speaker and Professional Certified Career Coach
Director/Founder Career Planning University

DISCOVER YOUR CAREER PASSION
http://www.careerplanningu.com

Contact information:
www.thetomjonesshow.com

Date:	Mon, 20 Jan 2003 14:30:51 -0800 (PST)
From:	"Gabe Kaplan" <gabe@gabekaplan.com>
Subject:	New Job Offer
To:	tjones@careerplanningu.com

Dear Tom,

Well the New Year has passed and I've gotten another job offer.

From reading my resume, I'd like you to give me one potential career choice you think is attainable along with its basic starting salary. If you are willing to do this, I could then decide whether to take this current offer or drop it and go ahead with you.

The latest offer is to be a guide for the boat tours of Ellis Island. They want me to wear immigrant clothing, circa 1880 (why do they always want me to dress up)? They said there's a small house on the island I could live in if I want.

At first I thought this could be exciting. It would be like seeing things through my grandparents' eyes, The Statue of Liberty and The New York skyline. Now I'm not so sure. My grandparents never had to live there, they were only there for one day, and as soon as they could afford it, they bought new clothes.

The New York City tour committee thinks that business would increase with me as the guide and they're willing to give me a share of that increase. They wont be specific as to what that share would be. The main guy Mr. Scarabino keeps saying, "don't worry, we're going to take care of you, you'll be happy."

He said I would get my picture taken with Mayor Bloomberg the day I started, but I would have to wear the immigrant garb.

What do you think, can you do better?

Gabe
gabe@gabekaplan.com

Date:	Tue, 21 Jan 2003 09:24:00 -0600
From:	"Tom (TJ) Jones" <tjones@careerplanningu.com>
Subject:	Re: New Job Offer
To:	gabe@gabekaplan.com

Nice to hear from you again. Let's see.... from actor, to muffin man to immigrant guide. Do you notice a pattern here Gabe? You're reaching for straws. No plan what so ever. Just opportunities. I'll teach you how to have a career plan. A map to your success. A guide to take you from Point A to Point B and beyond. I guarantee you.... no matter what job you took, you're not going to like it until you are sure, concise and clearly set on your career direction, goals and passion. And you are letting the "one's hiring" tell you what they'll do for you by saying "trust me". You don't want to make any decisions with an employer who doesn't also have a plan for you. My recommendation.... don't take anything until you know WHAT YOU WANT TO DO. And if you aren't sure, then that's why you need a career plan.

Here's what I'm going to propose. I think you are a perfect case study on the importance of career planning. You obviously will not pay me any fees to help you, so I'm willing to do something I would not normally do, but "you are a special case" and maybe we can help each other out and get a "win win" for both of us.

I'll work with you for 30 days. We'll have an initial conference call so we can establish a verbal relationship. You've already done the profile, so we are ready to go. At the end of 30 days, we can move onto another 30 days if you see progress. I'll take you through the 25 Steps to Your Ideal Career, a program I call DISCOVER YOUR CAREER PASSION. I wrote it and I'll take you through it one-on-one. I will help you develop a lifelong career plan and will charge you ..... ready for this??? **Nothing**....

That's right, I'll charge you nothing, in exchange for allowing me to use it as a case study. What that means is, you'll get notoriety for the case study in my new book and my national speaking tour. Heck, you might even accompany me on some of my speaking tours. What a great program... The Jew and the Christian talking about career planning. For someone like you, I'd probably charge at least $1000 per month, but if you'll let me help you, I'll defer all charges in exchange for the case study.

As a matter of fact, just to "wet your whistle", I believe you would make a great national speaker and we'll explore that idea through our teleconferences. You see, you're an actor. You're also independent. You also have "strange" habits and if you don't do things right and meet your personal goals and needs, you'll end up being used by people who won't respect you. You see, I'll use you.... but for the BETTER GOOD of millions of other people. They will learn the value of what you'll learn. You'll be used to HELP PEOPLE, not used by employers as the "thing to laugh at". You like laughs I know. That's you. I laugh all the time at your great comical comments. But laughing with you is different than laughing AT you. I want to get you to find a perfect career. And it may not be a typical 8-5 job. It may be an independent career that brings you happiness, success, money and you get to do what you LOVE.

Give me a chance. Let's work together and build this career plan for a lifetime. What do you have to lose? I'll do it free in exchange with helping me build a case study so you and I can help others overcome this frustrating problem. I'll even give you some royalties from the book. We may have an interesting thing going here.

Hope to hear back from you soon. I'm ready when you are.

Tom (TJ) Jones, PCCC, CPT
Author and National Speaker and Professional Certified Career Coach
Director/Founder Career Planning University

DISCOVER YOUR CAREER PASSION
http://www.careerplanningu.com

Contact information:
www.thetomjonesshow.com

Date:	Mon, 02 Dec 2002 13:55:04 -0800 (PST)
From:	"Gabe Kaplan" <gabe@gabekaplan.com>
Subject:	Coal Miner for a week
To:	dgibson@umwa.org

Dear Mr. Gibson:

Next year I will sit down and write my long-awaited book, "I've Done Everything." If you're not familiar with my story, since leaving television in 1983 I've taken a flyer at almost every profession imaginable. "Everything" will be loaded with pictures, stories, anecdotes, and even photocopied paychecks from all my different occupations. Sometimes the people knew who I was and what I was doing and sometimes they didn't. Some jobs I was actually good at, like carnival barker and seed salesman, while others got the better of me, like tollbooth attendant and hospital orderly.

To close out my saga I would like to be a coal miner for a week. What do I have to do? I'm a reasonably healthy fifty-seven year old man, so do you think I'll be able to take the grind and grime for that long? Is there Internet access during breaks? Do you still have to ride down in that rickety elevator? I'm not a prima donna; I just have a thing about shaky elevators.

Are there songs I have to learn? Does everybody bring his or her own canary? Sorry for all the questions, I'm just trying to find out what's involved.

Here's the best part from your end; I don't cash my paychecks. That's right, I work for free! It's all research for the book.

Ready to open my account at the company store,

Gabe Kaplan
gabe@gabekaplan.com

PS I once worked with Loretta Lynn in Reno.

Date:	Tue, 03 Dec 2002 09:23:35 -0500
From:	"Doug Gibson" <dgibson@umwa.org>
Subject:	Re: Coal Miner for a week
To:	gabe@gabekaplan.com

While I appreciate what you are doing, I have to tell you it might be difficult to get a one-week coal mining gig—although probably not impossible. It's really up to the coal operator as to whether or not you will be allowed to go underground. Due to your uneasiness with elevators, you may be better served working at a surface mine, although you lose a lot of the experience one gets when going underground. I was with Jesse Jackson on his first trip underground, and he referred to it as "a religious experience." Most of the elevators aren't rickety, but they aren't real smooth either. It's over quickly, if that helps. You also have a half-hour ride to the face on a mantrip too. Do you like rollarcoasters? Anyway, you will have to approach several different operators and hopefully end up at a mine with miners represented by the UMWA. For safety reasons, you should seek out a UMWA mine. Some of the larger operators are CONSOL, Peabody, Arch Coal and AEP. If you can get them to bite on your idea, you'll have to get safety training and probably sign a million releases. You'll also have to wear a red hard hat, which signifies "rookie miner." No, you won't have to learn any songs but you may want to adopt a nickname before one is attached to you by your co-workers, many of whom will probably have a lot of fun with you at your expense. Also if you have back problems, be prepared. Lots of hunching and even some crawling. Well, I hope this helps a little. Let me know how you are progressing. I love the premise of your book and I look forward to reading it and possibly reviewing it in our magazine.

Thanks

Doug Gibson

GERIATRIC PORNO STAR

Date:	Thu, 13 Nov 2003 14:14:52 -0800 (PST)
From:	"Gabe Kaplan" <gabe@gabekaplan.com>
Subject:	Unusual adult film
To:	dan@prophylacticpictures.com

Dear Dan,

For awhile now, I have had a project in mind, and thought you might be the perfect person to contact. This is something unique and groundbreaking: What if a mainstream television personality were to star in a hardcore adult film? What the heck- you've got to throw caution to the wind once in your life, take risks, do something unconventional. I've given this much thought, and if the proper deal can be struck, I would dive right in. I am between agents at this time, and would negotiate the particulars myself.

A possible story line would be a nice guy, in his mid-50's, who inherits a lot of money and for the first time, can have all the attractive, sexy women he has always desired. The kind of guy who's been in very few twosomes, and now he's doing threesomes, foursomes, and moresomes.

The "wood" element might be a small problem, but there's always Viagra and computer graphics. I think everyone involved could make out fabulously on this collaboration, although money is not my primary interest. I'd like to make a film with a message.

Sincerely,

Gabe Kaplan
gabe@gabekaplan.com

PS Attached is a picture taken earlier today

Date:	Fri, 14 Nov 2003 09:12:20 -0800
From:	"Dan" <dan@prophylacticpictures.com>
Subject:	Re: Unusual adult film
To:	gabe@gabekaplan.com

Gabe - I would be very interested in working with you on a ground breaking project such as this.

Please contact me on my cell at: 818-XXX-XXXX.

Dan

Date:	Tue, 28 Oct 2003 21:43:50 -0800 (PST)
From:	"Gabe Kaplan" <gabe@gabekaplan.com>
Subject:	Five Lunchdates
To:	dates@lunchdates.com

Dear Lunchdates,

I understand that the minimum is five Lunchdates for a charge of $680. So here is what I'm interested in. Tell me if you feel you can accommodate me.

Can you set me up with five women who are members of the extended Kennedy family? Now for the first time in thirty years I'm unattached. I feel akin to the Kennedys because of the similarities of our politics and lifestyles. I too live in a compound and am obsessed with social justice. I have been thinking about the political arena and what better way to enter it than with a Kennedy, Smith or Shriver at my side?

Unlike most men, I enjoy cuddling, long walks on the beach, and sharing feelings. As for my hobbies, I enjoy bowling, sailing, and photographing bighorn sheep. I'm able to do all this without leaving my compound.

In the event this relationship goes the distance, I prefer a civil ceremony to avoid any conflicts. I would get married in a church if necessary, but could not abide with any religious statues in my house.

Hope to hear from you soon,

Gabe Kaplan
gabe@gabekaplan.com

PS I enjoy a couple of drinks each evening but don't smoke.

Date:	Fri, 24 Oct 2003 16:49:48 -0700
From:	"Dates" <dates@lunchdates.com>
Subject:	Re: Question...
To:	gabe@gabekaplan.com

Gabe,

Complete the survey on our web site, and if we
feel we have women for you, we will contact you.

Steve

Gabe Kaplan

270 N Canon Drive, Suite 1404
Beverly Hills, CA 90210
gabe@gabekaplan.com

September 15, 2003

Kathy Brennan-Thompson
Chicken Soup for the Soul
PO Box 30880
Santa Barbara, CA 93130

Dear Ms. Brennan-Thompson,

I have read several of Dr. Canfield's Chicken Soup books and find them both inspirational and entertaining. The Chicken Soup office told me you are the person that handles new book proposals.

Since my television show left the airwaves some 25 years ago, I have basically been unemployed. I was not offered any good roles and chose not to do the junk that they do today.

Even when financially secure, most people feel compelled to have a job. They may despise what they do, but don't feel complete unless they're working.

Then there are those who refuse to punch in that time card unless they're doing something fulfilling. Some have financial resources and don't have to worry. Others would rather live a frugal existence than be forced into an unsatisfying profession.

The hard part seems to be getting family and friends to understand how you feel. One fellow told me his wife actually set up an intervention where his immediate circle, including a psychologist and a priest, tried to counsel him into going back to work. He said, "It was like one giant imitation of the Silhouettes, with everybody singing 'Get a job.'"

Would Dr. Canfield be interested in collaborating on a book, tentatively titled "Chicken Soup for the Purposely Unemployed"?

I have compiled over 150 great stories of proudly unemployed people that I would like to share with you and the doctor. It's amazing the things people can do with their lives if they have the time and insight to pursue their dreams. Let me know your thoughts.

Still unemployed,

Gabe
gabe@gabekaplan.com

PS Ironically one of the stories is about a dietician who specialized in soups. Several companies showed interest in his recipes. He refused to go along with their quality of ingredients and hasn't worked in four years. He has done amazing other things in this time period.

Date:	Wed, 22 Oct 2003 13:51:52 -0700
From:	"D'ette Corona" <dcorona@chickensoupbks.com>
Subject:	Chicken Soup for the Soul Proposal
To:	gabe@gabekaplan.com

Dear Gabe,

Thank you so much for proposing a new title for the Chicken Soup for the Soul® book series. Due to our production schedule or other similar titles already underway in our schedule, we must decline this proposal.

If you are not going to pursue this book concept on your own, we would love to consider including any stories you may have in one of our future book projects. Enclosed are the guidelines along with upcoming titles, should you wish to submit a story you have either written or collected.

We appreciate your enthusiastic interest in our work. It is the creative contributions by many, including yourself, who help us spread the light and achieve the goal of Changing the World One Story at a Time!

Please accept our best wishes for your success in your future endeavors.

Sincerely,

D'ette Corona
Co-author Liaison
Chicken Soup for the Soul Ent., Inc.

Date:	Wed, 22 Oct 2003 23:18:03 -0700 (PDT)
From:	"Gabe Kaplan" <gabe@gabekaplan.com>
Subject:	Chicken Soup for the Soul Proposal
To:	dcorona@chickensoupbks.com

Dear D'ette,

Unlike a clear bullion, chicken soup must move very slowly. I had pretty much given up on hearing from you. By the way, I did not receive the "Chicken Soup" guidelines, the titles, or even crackers. I did receive the upcoming releases, and the closest thing to my book was "Chicken Soup for Job Seekers" (the polar opposite of my idea). Are you saying you now have a project similar in theme to "Chicken Soup for the Purposely Unemployed"? Do we live in a parallel universe?

Since I didn't hear from you, I assumed you weren't interested in my idea; therefore I went about my business and now am close to completing the project. It is comprised of twenty-two stories written by purposely unemployed individuals who have found great joy and fulfillment in life, despite not working. I'm calling it: "Turkey Gumbo For People Who Hate Their Boss and Wish They Were Somewhere Else So They Wouldn't Have To Look At His Face Every Day." I wouldn't want to infringe upon Dr. Canfield's originality. Although Andy Warhol was into soup long before he was.

Can you send me your currently proposed title which you feel is similar in concept to my idea?

Best regards,

Gabe Kaplan
gabe@gabekaplan.com

PS "A bowl for me, a small cup for my friend" said the Dannite king.

Date:	Thu, 23 Oct 2003 08:26:40 -0700
From:	"D'ette Corona" <dcorona@chickensoupbks.com>
Subject:	Re: Chicken Soup for the Soul Proposal
To:	gabe@gabekaplan.com

Sorry for the delay in getting back to you and the confusion. I must first say, I am a big fan and excited that I am the person writing to you.

Due to the large number of Chicken Soup for the Soul books in the market place, our publisher reviews each proposed title and the market. Unfortunately our production schedules for 2005 and 2006 are already set and the publisher declined your proposal.

I wish you the best with your book.

D'ette

_____

D'ette Corona
Co-author Liaison
Chicken Soup for the Soul Ent., Inc.

Date: Fri, 24 Oct 2003 01:04:11 -0700 (PDT)
From: "Gabe Kaplan" <gabe@gabekaplan.com>
Subject: Re: Chicken Soup for the Soul Proposal
To: dcorona@chickensoupbks.com

Dear D'ette,

First let me say, I'm trilled you're such a big fan. If you're interested, I'm having a special this week on Gabe Kaplan mouse pads and coffee mugs.

As 'ole Mack once said to the Senate, "Let's cut to the chase." Do you now have a book scheduled for release similar in concept to "Chicken Soup For The Purposely Unemployed"? It doesn't matter if it's for 2005, 2006, or in the year 2525 (if man is still alive).

If you were simply sending me a polite rejection letter, I could accept that. On rare occasions, I have been rejected before. But your rejection seemed to include the possiblity of participating in a similar project. Sort of like when Francine DeNapoli said she didn't want to date me, but I could help her with her English homework.

Can you please tell me if you have a similar project to mine in the works?

Good luck to everybody- Dr. Canfield, Francine DeNapoli and you, the apostrophe lady.

Best regards,

Gabe
gabe@gabekaplan.com

PS Gabe Kaplan Mouse pads, $2.95.

Date:	Fri, 24 Oct 2003 09:30:45 -0700
From:	"D'ette Corona" <dcorona@chickensoupbks.com>
Subject:	Re: Chicken Soup for the Soul Proposal
To:	gabe@gabekaplan.com

I must say it was a polite form letter. Our
publisher is not onboard for your title.

D'ette Corona
Co-author Liaison
Chicken Soup for the Soul Ent., Inc.

Date:	Fri, 24 Oct 2003 13:35:12 -0700 (PDT)
From:	"Gabe Kaplan" <gabe@gabekaplan.com>
Subject:	Re: Chicken Soup for the Soul Proposal
To:	dcorona@chickensoupbks.com

Dear D'ette,

You didn't mention whether or not you want a mouse pad. It's too bad your publisher is not onboard for my title. I think I'll run it up the flagpole anyway. I appreciate you politesse. Basically, you were just trying to let aspiring authors down gently. I hope that part about you being a "fan" isn't part of the form letter.

Best wishes,

Gabe
gabe@gabekaplan.com

Date:	Fri, 24 Oct 2003 14:30:00 -0700
From:	"D'ette Corona" <dcorona@chickensoupbks.com>
Subject:	Re: Chicken Soup for the Soul Proposal
To:	gabe@gabekaplan.com

I would love the mouse pad and was serious about being a big fan.

Take care

D'ette Corona
Co-author Liaison
Chicken Soup for the Soul Ent., Inc.

Date: Mon, 10 Mar 2003 21:24:49 -0800 (PST)
From: "Gabe Kaplan" <gabe@gabekaplan.com>
Subject: Question about the library
To: robert@lbjlib.utexas.edu

Dear Mr. Hicks,
Johnson Library,

What did Magic Johnson have to do with Texas and why is his library located there? I know he's from Michigan and played his whole career for the Lakers in Los Angeles. He always beat up on the Spurs, the Rockets, and the Mavericks pretty good, so I don't know why you would want his library in the Lone Star state. I guess there was that time when the Rockets bounced the Lakers in the first round back in '81, Magic's sophomore year, but I don't have to tell you that. Was Magic born in Austin? He must have been, that's the only thing that makes sense.

Before I make the trip to your city could you tell me a little bit about some of the exhibits and merchandise you have available? How many books has Magic written? Does your library also include books that Magic has read? Do you have any tapes from his great television talk show? How many of the "Showtime" Lakers have visited the library? How often does Magic drop by? Again, it would make so much more sense if his library were in LA. I just can't get over the fact that it's in Austin, Texas.

I have a picture of your guy and myself taken at the Laker training camp in Hawaii in 1988. Is this an item you might possibly want? Please get back to me at your earliest convenience.

Gabe Kaplan

Date:	Tue, 11 Mar 2003 14:29:01 -0600
From:	"Robert Hicks" <robert@lbjlib.utexas.edu>
Subject:	Re: Question about the library
To:	gabe@gabekaplan.com

Mr. Kaplan,

This is the Lyndon Baines Johnson Library
and Museum, one of 10 Presidential Libraries
across the United States. Although we have
no objects about Magic, you should still come
and visit Austin and tour our museum.

Robert Hicks
LBJ Library and Museum

Date:	Wed, 12 Mar 2003 20:24:20 -0800 (PST)
From:	"Gabe Kaplan" <gabe@gabekaplan.com>
Subject:	Re: Question about the library
To:	robert@lbjlib.utexas.edu

Robert,

How silly of me not to realize your library was devoted to *Lyndon* Johnson. If I ever am in Austin, I will definitely stop by. Can you ask Ladybird if she would like to put the attached picture of Magic and me in the library anyway? It might make a good conversation piece.

Date:	Sat, 05 Apr 2003 13:32:19 -0800 (PST)
From:	"Gabe Kaplan" <gabe@gabekaplan.com>
Subject:	New "Kotter" opera
To:	gockley@hopera.org

Dear Mr. Gockley,

My most informed opera aficionados have told me that your company might be the one to experiment with a new and unique piece. I have spent the past three years writing a "Welcome Back Kotter" opera in Italian. In order to make this possible, I have spent the better part of two years in Italy and South Jersey just learning the language and customs. This project was just a crazy sogno.

Imagine the beloved characters of one of television's classic sitcoms, singing and emoting in classic operatic style. Just to whet your appetite with a bocconcino of the plot: Kotter finds out he is the product of an illegitimate relationship between his mother and Mr. Woodman (the school principal). Miss Fishbeck, the scellarata, exposes this scandal which drives Mr. Kotter to the verge of suicide. His aria at the end of the first act is a show-stopper.

Another poignant moment occurs when Horschack quits school and finds work as a melancholy circus clown, which in addition to being quite touching, should save you some money on a costume.

If you have a sincere interest in the project, I will send you a complete tape of the piece, performed in my apartment by most of the original T.V. cast. Don't worry, I just used them to make the tape. When the time comes, I can let them go.

Sincere regards,

Gabe Kaplan

PS A dinner opera house in Arizona is willing to mount the production for four weeks. Would you recommend this as a way of getting the piece on its feet?

Date:	Mon, 07 Apr 2003 12:07:10 -0500
From:	"Mary Fanidi" <mfanidi@hopera.org>
Subject:	Re: New "Kotter" opera
To:	gabe@gabekaplan.com

Dear Mr. Kaplan:

If you will be good enought to send us a piano vocal and libretto we would be happy to review it.

Kind regards,

Mary Fanidi
Office of the General Director
Houston Grand Opera

Date:	Tue, 08 Apr 2003 12:06:47 -0500
From:	"Mary Fanidi" <mfanidi@hopera.org>
Subject:	Dear Mr. Kaplan:
To:	gabe@gabekaplan.com

Dear Mr. Kaplan:

David Gockley asked that I respond regarding the dinner opera house in Arizona. It can be useful as an opportunity to work out issues and any problems, he said.

Kind regards,
Mary Fanidi
Office of the General Director
Houston Grand Opera

Date:	Thu, 10 Apr 2003 22:22:47 -0700 (PDT)
From:	"Gabe Kaplan" <gabe@gabekaplan.com>
Subject:	Dear Ms. Fanidi
To:	mfanidi@hopera.org

Dear Mary,

Thank you and Mr. Gockley very much for taking the time to reply and for the offer to review my piece. I have taken Mr. Gockley's advice and booked the Arizona dinner opera theater. Then, as you say in Houston, I can "fuss" with it a little before sending you the piano vocals and libretto.

All the original "Sweathogs" are on for Arizona except for Mr. Big Shot (I'm not sure his voice would measure up anyway). Unfortunately, John Sylvester White, the principal, has passed away. Do you have any thoughts on a possible Mr. Woodman? Carreras would be perfect. Do you think it's possible he would do this on a lark?

Best Regards,

Gabe Kaplan

Date:	Fri, 11 Apr 2003 14:04:17 -0500
From:	"Mary Fanidi" <mfanidi@hopera.org>
Subject:	Re: Dear Ms. Fanidi
To:	gabe@gabekaplan.com

Dear Mr. Kaplan:

David replies that chances are remote that
Carreras would accept. He sings very little
these days and when he does he gets big money.

John Duykers, Matthew Lord or Joey Evans may be
possible candidates to consider for the role of
Mr. Woodman.

Hope this is helpful.

Regards,
Mary

Date:	Fri, 11 Apr 2003 12:58:14 -0700 (PDT)
From:	"Gabe Kaplan" <gabe@gabekaplan.com>
Subject:	Thanks for your help
To:	mfanidi@opera.org

Dear Mary,

Thanks so much for your assistance. I'll be in touch with you after Arizona.

Regards,

Gabe

Date:	Fri, 11 Apr 2003 15:01:56 -0500
From:	"Mary Fanidi" <mfanidi@hopera.org>
Subject:	Re: Thanks for your help
To:	gabe@gabekaplan.com

Hope it is successful..

It really helps to see it on its feet - and work out the cliches.

Date:	Tue, 10 Jun 2003 11:07:55 -0700 (PDT)
From:	"Gabe Kaplan" <gabe@gabekaplan.com>
Subject:	New Rasputin Play
To:	alex@disinfo.com

Dear Mr. Burns,

Your website talks about some of the misinformation about Rasputin. I am in the process of developing a theatrical project entitled "Raspy and Unpredictable." It chronicles the lighter side of "The Mad Monk."

Let me start out by telling you some things I've heard. Things that are not in any of the Rasputin books or reference materials. For instance, I've been told that he did impressions. His Nijinsky was supposedly dead-on.

Also, all the comedy hypnotists of the last 90 years owe their livelihood to his trail-blazing work. I've heard that one time he hypnotized the entire Czar's court and got them acting like drunken, sex-crazed Polish soldiers.

Speaking of sex, in your opinion what is the truth about his relationship with the Czarina and was there anything amusing about it? Remember, funny is what I'm looking for. Have you heard that he met with a teen-aged Eleanor Roosevelt when she visited Moscow with her high school rhythmic gymnastics team? I'm not sure if this is based on reality or just wild speculation.

Was he really able to change the color of his eyes at will? Or, do you think, as is rumored, he had access to early contact lenses, a la Lon Chaney Sr.? And, in your opinion, did he really have no concern for personal hygiene or was that just his "hook?"

The climactic comedy scene will, of course, be the assassination. After all, what could be funnier than trying to kill a guy eight different ways and the mofo refuses to cash in his chips? Write me back soon so we can share information and I can start sending you some completed pages. I hope you're not offended that I intend to do a comedy on his life.

Cyanide-a,

Gabe Kaplan
gabe@gabekaplan.com

PS I'm taking some Rasputin pictures tomorrow. Could I send you one so you can critique it?

Date:	Wed, 11 Jun 2003 21:39:35 +1000
From:	"Alex Burns" <alex@disinfo.com>
Subject:	Re: New Rasputin Play
To:	gabe@gabekaplan.com

Gabe,

I've not looked at Rasputin's material in 18 months, but you've definitely got some good ideas for your play. The Roosevelt story is speculation.

He may also have had access to early contact lenses, possible. His influence on latter-day comedian hypnotists may be the play's selling point.

Alex

—

Alex Burns
alex@disinfo.com

Alex,

Rasputin has gotten a lot of attention in the last 18 months. He's hot. Everybody is writing about him. I think there is a lot of misinformation going around.

What speculation have you heard about the Roosevelt situation? I heard she carried a picture of "The Mad Monk" for 20 years, until Lorena Hickok made her destroy it around 1936. Supposedly, Franklin found the picture amusing.

You're right about the comedy hypnotist thing being a good hook. He *was* and *is* comedy hypnotism. In fact, the New York theatrical agents had a phrase to describe each form of variety entertainment. An agent would say, "I need three hoofers, two crooners, and one comic Rasputin for a job."

I'm attaching one of the digital pictures we took, any input about how authentic looking it is would be greatly appreciated.

Thanks for your help.

Gabe
gabe@gabekaplan.com

PS There was a guy in London named Leonard Zelig who worked for 20 years as a comedy hypnotist under the name "Leon Rasputin." He claimed to be Raspy's cousin. Zelig was once introduced to Anna Tchaikovski, she disputed his claim and thought he was crazy. I would have loved to have been a fly on the wall that evening.

39 I ALWAYS INHALE

Date: Tue, 17 Jun 2003 20:50:35 -0700 (PDT)
From: "Gabe Kaplan" <gabe@gabekaplan.com>
Subject: Pot Is Better Than Booze
To: ocbc@rxcbc.org

Dear Oakland Cannabis Buyers Cooperative,

If you talk to me about legalizing marijuana you're preaching to the choir. This is something that should've been done a long time ago. There are bars and liquor stores in every neighborhood. Alcohol has ruined more lives and caused more traffic accidents than pot. Most alcohol tastes bad and the people that drink it smell bad. Pot smells good. And then they also sell cigarettes, which studies have shown are terrible for people and their lungs. But if someone just wants to light up a joint in the privacy of his or her home, Big Brother steps in. Alcohol is bad for your liver and your kidneys but pot makes your whole body mellow out.

This letter is just to tell you that I support what you're doing. And I'm not even a big pothead. I've smoked consistently but always recreationally and never addictedly. Nobody's forced to do anything in my house. Most of the time we just mellow out "on the natch." Some of my best friends are vegetarians and I, myself, won't eat sushi. After casual smoking for 40 years, I feel as sharp as I ever was, particularly on questions about movies and awards and which year they were won.

You know you can see these anti-pot people and their attitudes fitting in with the '50s and '60s. But now that we're past the '90s you'd think they'd stop all their bullshit. It's okay for them to get drunk every night but we can't kick back the way we want.

Here's a new topical bumper sticker: "Admit you inhale."

Gabe Kaplan
gabe@gabekaplan.com

PS I'm going to be in Oakland for the first Raider game of the season. Can I call you when I'm in town?

Date:	Wed, 18 Jun 2003 11:46:53 -0700
From:	"OCBC Staff" <ocbc@rxcbc.org>
Subject:	Re: Pot Is Better Than Booze
To:	gabe@gabekaplan.com

Dear Gabe:

Thanks very much for your support and
testimonial. Please check out our web site,
especially the links page, for opportunities for
involvement.

Date:	Wed, 18 Jun 2003 20:31:18 -0700 (PDT)
From:	"Gabe Kaplan" <gabe@gabekaplan.com>
Subject:	Hulk Opens Friday
To:	ocbc@rxcbc.org

Dear OCBC,

No problem. I have time to check out all those web sites. Basically I've got nothing to do until Friday. That's the big day when The Hulk opens. I've been looking forward to it for weeks. I'm sure I'll sit through at least two shows. That should be a trip! I saw Shrek three times the day it opened. It was great, it reminded me of Pinocchio. I loved Pinocchio, but there was something weird about it. I don't know what Walt Disney was into, but it wasn't pot.

Thanks for the offer to link up when I'm in Oakland. Go Raiders!

Gabe
gabe@gabekaplan.com

PS Can you send me the names of the countries where grass is legal? I know Amsterdam is one.

Date: Fri, 20 Jun 2003 22:09:51 -0700 (PDT)
From: "Gabe Kaplan" <gabe@gabekaplan.com>
Subject: Saw It!
To: ocbc@rxcbc.org

Dear OCBC Staff:

Saw it twice. I actually liked it better the second time. I'm going to try and go again Sunday with my 13 year old daughter. She wants to see "Alex and Emma" so I'm going to have to talk her out of that and onto "The Hulk".

Can you answer my question as to what countries grass is legal in? I'm going to London in August and then maybe I'll go to Europe. I won't go to Turkey or any place like that. I saw "Round Midnight". Scary movie. Do you know that the same actor who was in that movie played a runner in "Chariots of Fire"?

Sorry to bother you with this. If I could use the internet beyond email, this information is probably available. What about the Scandanavian countries including Iceland? Is it legal there?

Gabe
gabe@gabekaplan.com

Date:	Mon, 30 Jun 2003 22:55:06 -0700 (PDT)
From:	"Gabe Kaplan" <gabe@gabekaplan.com>
Subject:	Wednesday is Terminator 3
To:	ocbc@rxcbc.org

Dear OCBC Staff:

How come you don't answer about the countries grass is legal in? Remember, the key word here is "legal".

Well, you know what Wednesday is! The day our next governor of California debuts in Terminator 3. I can't wait! This is probably the last one. What if Arnold was governor for one term and then came back and made T4. You know who would be the classic villain? The guy that's been behind the Terminator planet from the beginning: Jesse Ventura! How's that for casting?

Do you think this would be a funny cartoon: Arnold is wearing a "Recall" T-shirt, walks by Grey Davis and says "Hasta La Vista, Baby". I know you probably like Grey Davis but it would be a funny cartoon.

If you give me that list of legal grass countries, I promise I won't bother you anymore with my jokes and movie premieres. You've probably got it lying around there somewhere and I don't know who else to ask.

Best Regards,

Gabe Kaplan
gabe@gabekaplan.com

PS How many of you are old enough to remember when grass was called "tea"?

Date:	Tue, 01 Jul 2003 10:35:50 -0700
From:	"OCBC Staff" <ocbc@rxcbc.org>
Subject:	Re: Wednesday is Terminator 3
To:	gabe@gabekaplan.com

Hello Gabe
You can always send email to us, not all if it
may be read or responded to but we try to keep
up.

I don't think we have a list of grass countries,
you best hope would be to contact California
NORML at www.canorml.org, grass as tea, hmm i
like cannabis better, even though I'm a tea
drinker

Date: Wed, 07 May 2003 11:31:31 -0700 (PDT)
From: "Gabe Kaplan" <gabe@gabekaplan.com>
Subject: Reviewing "Girls Gone Wild" Movie
To: bill@mantent.com

Dear Bill,

As you may be aware, I am now the movie reviewer for *Senior Entertainment Weekly*. One of my upcoming assignments is to review your "Girls Gone Wild" movie prior to its release.

In the interest of fairness, I would like to tell you that you might find my name on your mail order list since in the past I have purchased videos.

I bought "Girls Gone Wild" expecting to see wild girls in trees and caves, wild girls foraging for food, and wild girls roaming in packs on the Serengeti. For two weeks I anxiously awaited the arrival of the videos. I couldn't get those wild girls and the fantasies they created out of my head.

When the video finally arrived I went in my room, locked the door, ripped open the package and, inserted the tape in my VCR. What a disappointment. All I saw was young women exposing their breasts and private parts in sleazy urban settings. And then you have scenes of these women kissing each other. Like any senior wants to see that. If you ever make a video with truly wild girls, let me know.

Wild thing, you make my heart sing,

Gabe Kaplan
gabe@gabekaplan.com

PS If you would prefer that someone else review the movie, I can forward that request to my editors at the magazine.

Date:	Wed, 07 May 2003 12:14:13 -0700
From:	"Bill" <bill@mantent.com>
Subject:	Re: Reviewing "Girls Gone Wild" Movie
To:	gabe@gabekaplan.com

Gabe

I'd be happy to send you are new title when it's ready. I just need a physical address.

- Bill

Date:	Wed, 07 May 2003 12:39:31 -0700 (PDT)
From:	"Gabe Kaplan" <gabe@gabekaplan.com>
Subject:	Re: Reviewing "Girls Gone Wild" Movie
To:	bill@mantent.com

Bill,

Thank you for your prompt and courteous reply. Yes, please send me you new title. If you don't mind, I would like to review the movie for the magazine myself. I'm sure it's going to be different than the videos. Can I give my editors some idea of when you expect to have the new title? Being older, we like to plan our publications far in advance.

Here is my physical address:

Gabe Kaplan
270 N. Canon Dr.
Suite 1404
Beverly Hills, CA 90210

Gabe
gabe@gabekaplan.com

Date:	Wed, 07 May 2003 12:54:56 -0700
From:	"Bill" <bill@mantent.com>
Subject:	Re: Reviewing "Girls Gone Wild" Movie
To:	gabe@gabekaplan.com

may

Date:	Wed, 07 May 2003 12:55:08 -0700
From:	"Bill" <bill@mantent.com>
Subject:	Re: Reviewing "Girls Gone Wild" Movie
To:	gabe@gabekaplan.com

Late may, actually

Date:	Wed, 20 Aug 2003 14:31:33 -0700 (PDT)
From:	"Gabe Kaplan" <gabe@gabekaplan.com>
Subject:	Re: Reviewing "Girls Gone Wild" Movie
To:	bill@mantent.com

Bill:

I received your new "Girls Gone Wild" video and towel. Thank you for sending them.

I brought the video to my senior kite boarding club. I wanted to see how they liked it. One old geezer became so excited I think he went and relieved himself in the broom closet (don't worry, I wouldn't let him use your towel) However, like me, the rest of the guys felt uncomfortable. We don't mind looking at a beautiful woman, but the girls in your video are the same age as our granddaughters.

Here's an idea that you might pass on to your bosses or whoever makes the decisions: To get men of all ages excited, how about a video called "Movie Matrons Gone Wild"? Every male gets excited at the thought of a sexy, mature movie matron in a starched white uniform. I guarantee it would be your biggest seller ever. Granted, they would not be able to flash as quickly as they young girls. Layers of clothing would have to be removed. More of a buildup.

Instead of Snoop Dogg, I could be the guy that talks these ladies into "getting nekked." We could film them in the manager's office, next to the candy machine or by the fountain in the lobby. How about two movie matrons doing each other on the balcony. Talk about hot, Wow-e-Wow.

Gabe
gabe@gabekaplan.com

PS Let me know if the GGW movie project is still in the works. My editors at SEW asked me about it.

Date:	Sat, 23 Aug 2003 11:35:22 -0700
From:	"Bill" <bill@mantent.com>
Subject:	Re: Is Movie Still On?
To:	gabe@gabekaplan.com

the movie is still on. waiting for script ok

Gabe Kaplan

270 N Canon Drive, Suite 1404
Beverly Hills, CA 90210
gabe@gabekaplan.com

May 29, 2003

Southwest Airlines
Customer Relations
P.O. Box 36647 – 1CR
Dallas, TX 75235-1647

Dear Southwest Airlines,

Your carrier is my favorite. I really appreciate your flight crew's positive attitude, and I love the flight attendants' funny jokes. My favorite is, "Please pay particular attention to the following announcement if you're seated next to a child or someone who is acting like a child."

Last year, you instituted a policy that severely obese people have to pay two fares, one adult and one child. My question is one that your sales agents did not seem to be able to answer: does your rule apply to obese celebrities as well? People from whose patronage you benefit indirectly? Like when someone says, "Guess who I flew with on Southwest Airlines last week? Louie Anderson! Boy that was exciting!" That benefits you.

They say a picture is worth a thousand words. Enclosed please find a photo of me taken two weeks ago. It's a long story; don't ask. I quit smoking, started drinking, and became hooked on Krispy Kreme donuts. The more my career fizzled, the more Krispy Kremes I ate. Have you ever tried the chocolate custard? Yesterday, I tipped the scales at a svelte 326. Most of it, unfortunately, filtering its way down to my hips and butt. This massive weight gain has brought on a severe depression for which my antidepressant pills are more Krispy Kremes. The outlook is bleak.

My only solace comes from my twice-monthly trips to Las Vegas where I play blackjack and poker with my friends. Even this has its dark side. People are constantly coming up and telling me that I look like a fat Gabe Kaplan.

I love to eat and it shows,

Gabe Kaplan
gabe@gabekaplan.com

PS Last week I was taking off on a flight from Vegas to LAX. The flight attendant said she was tired of handing out peanuts, so we would have to grab our own. She then put about 30 packs on the carpet and the packages ran all the way down the aisles as the plane ascended. Everybody was hysterical.

SOUTHWEST AIRLINES CO.

Brian Lusk
Manager
Executive Office Customer Communications

Love Field
P.O. Box 36611
Dallas, TX 75235-1611

July 7, 2003

330480

Mr. Gabe Kaplan
Suite 1404
270 North Canon Drive
Beverly Hills, CA 90210

Dear Mr. Kaplan:

I've often wondered what it would have been like to be in the meeting where they designed the doughnut. Who came up with the bright idea to remove the center? Oh well, if they hadn't invented the doughnut hole, we all would probably be eating doughblobs—just doesn't have the same meaning, though. However, I find temptation extremely hard to resist, and if Krispy Kreme sold doughblobs, I would be hooked! (If *Variety* wrote about an increase of Krispy Kreme sales, would the headline be, "Dough Shop does Boffo BO"? My mind has always reeled at the thought of "boffo BO," but I am a bit twisted.)

Anyway, we are excited that Southwest is your favorite airline, and hearing praise for our folks' sense of humor from someone as talented as you makes the praise just that sweeter—no pun intended. Shame on those "showbiz moguls" if they think otherwise, because it takes true talent right from the heart to be able to equate Louie Anderson with "exciting."

Unfortunately, our Customer of Size policy must apply to all Customers, even "obese celebrities." (Incidentally, the determining factor on whether a Customer needs to purchase an extra seat is if the Customer can't sit comfortably in the seat with the armrest down.) It just wouldn't be right to let fame, talent, or fortune exempt one person and not the other. I hope you understand.

Here's hoping that the Vegas tables are kind and that we see you on many more flights to come!

Sincerely,

Brian Lusk

/bl

207

Gabe Kaplan

270 N. CANON DRIVE #1404
BEVERLY HILLS, CA 90210
gabe@gabekaplan.com

October 7, 2006

ALLISON KLIMMERMAN
COLGATE/PALMOLIVE
CORPORATE COMMUNICATIONS DEPT
300 PARK AVENUE
NEY YORK, NY 10022

Dear Ms. Klimmerman,

Next month I'll be shooting a comedy pilot for cable television called "Over Sixty and Still Frisky." It's about love and romance among the residence of the Kakamon retirement home in North Palm Beach, FL.

On the pilot episode, Mrs. Mandlebaum played by Bea Arthur and Mrs. Nakano played by Rita Moreno, are arguing over the affections of Mr. Cheese played by Tom Poston. One says to the other, "Why would he schtup you, you're older than Palmolive soap?"

We would like to make this a running gag if the series gets picked up. Not the "Schtup" part, just the "You're older than Palmolive soap." At least once a week, someone will use that catch phrase. If it catches on, the whole country could start using it. Sort of like "You're slower than Heinz ketchup."

Please let me know if there are any legal objections before we shoot the pilot.

Gabe Kaplan

PS In writing the name, I noticed for the first time it's a combination of the words Palm and Olive. Do you know what the significance of this was?

COLGATE-PALMOLIVE COMPANY
A Delaware Corporation

300 Park Avenue
New York, NY 10022
Telephone 212-
Fax 212-

Felicia G. Traub
Associate Counsel, Trademark & Copyright
Trademark

December 12, 2002

Mr. Gabe Kaplan
270 N. Canon Drive #1404
Beverly Hills, CA 90210

Re: Request for use of PALMOLIVE trademark in Television Pilot
        "Over Sixty and Still Frisky"

Dear Mr. Kaplan:

Allison Klimmerman of Colgate-Palmolive Company's (hereinafter, "CPC") Corporate Communications Department forwarded to me your letter of November 22, 2002, in which you seek CPC's permission to use the renowned trademark PALMOLIVE in your comedy pilot.

You have explained your desire to use the PALMOLOVE mark in the line "Why would he schtup you, you're older than Palmolive soap?" and also as a catch phrase, "You're older than Palmolive soap," throughout the series.

We hereby inform you that CPC does not authorize you to use the PALMOLIVE mark in this manner in your comedy show.

We thank you for contacting us and trust that you will respect CPC's position. We wish you much luck in your new entertainment endeavor.

Very truly yours,

Felicia G. Traub

Wilma
(Somewhere in the
Southern United States)

January 26, 2003

Ms. Gabriel Kaplan

Dear Ms. Kaplan:
I am writing you because I am a fan of yours, and I have long admired your talents.
I want you thank you for your many contributions to acting in our popular culture.
I was wondering if you would mind sending me a personalized autographed photograph. I would be very proud to add it to my wonderful collection of Actress's.
I hope to hear from you soon and deeply appreciate your generosity in fulfilling this request.
Thank you in advance for your kindness.

Sincerely
Wilma
Wilma

Date:	Fri, 31 Jan 2003 12:09:55 -0800 (PST)
From:	"Gabe Kaplan" <gabe@gabekaplan.com>
Subject:	Received your autograph request
To:	wilma@southfan.net

Dear Wilma,

When I received your letter today I was shocked. How could you, living in the south, possibly known what happened at the hospital? You must have a relative who works there. You know they all signed confidentiality agreements so who ever told you shouldn't have.

Since you know I must count on your discretion. This is not public knowledge!

Did your informer tell you I went in there just for hip replacement surgery? That's it, a hip, nothing else was supposed to be replaced or eliminated. You always hear about mistakes being made at hospitals, but you never think it can happen to you.

People tell me I might have a case for a lawsuit, but how do you put a financial value on what I lost? The trail would be too embarrassing. I'm sure my ex wife would have something to say in court as to its worth.

It seems to me you want to be the first person to get the new publicity photo. Well I'm not taken them for at least two weeks. I've got to be completely comfortable with the new "me" first. It still feels like I've lost a friend.

Best regards,

Gabriel Kaplan
gabe@gabekaplan.com

PS To add insult to injury they never replaced the hip.

Dear Ms. Kaplan,
I am really confussed, I wrote you a letter but
it was just asking for you autograph, that is
it. I am being very honest with you, I could'nt
tell you what you were in the hospital for.
You have been a fan of mine for years, I think
of you as on of the great actress, Love you in
Lewis and Clark and Welcome Back Kotter.

I asure you I have no family members working at
any hospital, so not you just relax and don't
worry about me saying anything about something
that I don't even know about. Your one of my
heros.

Please keep in touch.
What ever it was I wish you great health, and
all is better.

Your fan,
Wilma

Date:	Sat, 15 Feb 2003 14:40:11 -0600
From:	"Wilma" <wilma@southfan.net>
Subject:	GASOLINE SOLUTION!
To:	gabe@gabekaplan.com

Dear Mo. Kaplan,

GASOLINE SOLUTION!
We CAN buy gasoline that's not from Middle East.
Gas rationing in the 80's worked even though we
grumbled about it. It might even be good for us!

The Saudis are boycotting American goods. We should
return the favor. An interesting thought is to boycott
their GAS. Every time you fill up the car, you can
avoid putting more money into the coffers of Saudi
Arabia. Just buy from gas companies that don't import
their oil from the Saudis.

Nothing is more frustrating than the feeling that
every time I fill-up the tank, I am sending my money
to people who are trying to kill me, my family, and
my friends. I thought it might be interesting for
you to know which oil companies are the best to buy
gas from and which major companies import.

Middle Eastern oil (for the period 9/1/00 - 8/31/01):
Shell......................205,742,000 barrels
Chevron/Texaco........144,332,000 barrels
Exxon /Mobil...............130,082,000 barrels
Marathon/Speedway...117,740,000 barrels
Amoco......................62,231,000 barrels
If you do the math at $30/barrel, these imports
amount to over $18 BILLION!

Here are some large companies that "do not" import
Middle Eastern oil:
Citgo...................0 barrels
Sunoco............. ..0 barrels
Conoco............. ..0 barrels
Sinclair.............. 0 barrels
BP/Phillips.......... 0 barrels
Hess..................0 barrels

Date:	Tue, 18 Feb 2003 10:41:35 -0800
From:	"Gabe Kaplan" <gabe@gabekaplan.com>
Subject:	New Photos Next Week
To:	wilma@southfan.net

Dear Wilma:

I received your latest email. It was very interesting seeing which gas companies do and do not use Mid-East oil. As you requested, I've forwarded it to ten people, including Jamie Farr, she's very political about the Mid-East.

Knowing that you've always considered me a great actress makes what's happened easier to handle. Destiny is a funny thing and I believe you're subtly telling me we don't control our own. We have to play the cards we've been dealt, whatever they are.

The new photos are going to be taken next week and you will be one of the first to get one. Today I'm going shopping for a spring wardrobe at the Big-N-Tall Gal's store. I'm completely comfortable with the new me, and if people don't like it, nuts to them.

Remember, till the pictures come out, mums the word!

Thanks for the support, girlfriend.

Best regards,

Gabriel
gabe@gabekaplan.com

Date:	Tue, 18 Feb 2003 21:57:23 -0600
From:	"Wilma" <wilma@southfan.net>
Subject:	Re: New Photos Next Week
To:	gabe@gabekaplan.com

You got it, and thank you for writing me I
really enjoy that.

Wilma

Date:	Sun, 01 Jun 2003 19:49:55 -0700 (PDT)
From:	"Gabe Kaplan" <gabe@gabekaplan.com>
Subject:	Amy's Story, Sunday Tea and There's No Laughing In Baseball
To:	wilma@southfan.net

Wilma,

Attached, please find the new picture. It's Sunday and I have just come back from high tea at the Coliseum Trailer Park. Some of the gals there are in my same situation (ex-truck drivers and servicemen). We enjoy having tea, cucumber sandwiches, and chatting together. Of course, their current gender status is voluntary and mine was accidental.

This still makes me a little different. Today I asked if we could put on the Dodger game. They all laughed like it was a joke. That hurt me deeply.

Can you believe that two of them have boyfriends already? I don't even want to think about that. Men usually keep their distance from me. I don't know what I'd do if some guy made a pass at me.

Maybe I could come South and spend a few days with you. I'll stay in a hotel if you don't have room. I just have to get away.

Gabriel
gabe@gabekaplan.com

PS Do you enjoy watching baseball? You're probably a Braves fan. I hope they aren't playing the Dodgers when I visit.

Wilma:

Unfortunately, I haven't heard from you so I'm going to take a vacation in Maine and see my sister for about a week. Maybe I'll come to see you some other time. This will be the first time I have traveled since my surgery. I'm a little apprehensive, but excited as well.

Why haven't you written back? Did my picture scare you?

Gabriel
gabe@gabekaplan.com

Date:	Mon, 27 Jan 2003 22:54:44 -0800 (PST)
From:	"Gabe Kaplan" <gabe@gabekaplan.com>
Subject:	Normadic Ex-TV Star
To:	brent@enrichyoulife.com

Dear Brent:

Your website is fascinating. I'm wondering if you think you can help me with my problem.

For fifteen years I have not worked anywhere in the western world. My exile started when a U.K. critic said that my jokes were so bad he would like to ring my neck like a chicken. Some chicken! Some neck! That's why I have not been visible on American television. Thankfully I speak eight languages and have been able to find comedy clubs in other places.

From Stettin in the Baltic to Trieste in the Adriatic, my comedy curtain has descended over Eastern Europe. The people there love my jokes, they remember my television show and are impressed that I speak their language. The critics love me too; one in Belgrade commented that all I give my audiences are laughs, blood, toil, tears and sweat.

You ask, what is my aim? I can answer in one word. Laughter - Laughter at all costs - Laughter in spite of all terrors - Laughter, however long and hard the road may be, for without Laughter there is no survival for me.

Although I still get laughs, the yearning to tell a joke in English is overwhelming. I need the self esteem to brace myself for my final duty, to perform on an American stage again. If you can help me do this and the tape of that show last for a thousand years, men will still say, "This was his finest and funniest hour."

My question to you is, can we say the past is the past without surrendering the future?

Gabe Kaplan
gabe@gabekaplan.com

Date:	Tue, 25 Feb 2003 16:16:22 -0800
From:	"Brent" <brent@enrichyoulife.com>
Subject:	Confidence Mentoring
To:	gabe@gabekaplan.com

Gabe,

I can definitely help you. We'll have you more
confident than you dreamed in no time.

There will be an abundance of laughter after
we work together. You'll have your "funniest
hours".

I guarantee your results.

I don't normally do mentoring but for you I'm
going to offer you a private mentoring special:

*unlimited access to me via phone, fax, and email
*access to my VIP private telephone number
*technology developed from advanced research and
application (you can redevelop the technology
but it would take 5-6 years, hundreds of books
of research, tens of thousands of dollars, and
much trial and error)

I require a three month minimum for my program.
The investment is $2857 US dollars.

You'll get unlimited access to me for three months.

Let me know how you soon you want to get started
and getting your confidence that you deserve back.

warmly,
Brent

Date:	Wed, 26 Feb 2003 19:34:06 -0800 (PST)
From:	"Gabe Kaplan" <gabe@gabekaplan.com>
Subject:	letter
To:	brent@enrichyoulife.com

Dear Brent,

Please forgive the impertinence of my responding to your proposal to Mr. Kaplan. My name is John Martin and I am his principle private secretary. I prepare the yearly honours list, and call the roll when he's away.

Currently he in on a six week comedy club tour of Albania. His final stop will be at Salty's in Tirana. Last time there he broke the Friday late show record.

Brent, he does so want to perform in English again and I would hate to see him disappointed another time. Do you feel confident you can help him?

He spent hours on hours talking to that Jamaican lady on the phone at 4.99 per minute. He also bought the Charles Atlas book and started working out. So many things have been tried to boost his self confidence and none of them seem to work.

Is there any guarantee that after engaging your system, Mr. Kaplan will be able to tell jokes in English again. Could we work out a deal where if he works at least one week you get paid a little more, if not you get much less.

John Martin

Date:	Wed, 12 Mar 2003 21:48:15 -0800 (PST)
From:	"Gabe Kaplan" <gabe@gabekaplan.com>
Subject:	Back home, must apologize
To:	brent@enrichyoulife.com

Dear Brent,

I have just returned from my concert tour. It seems that in my absence my assistant, John Martin, had the effrontery to write you on my behalf. I am shocked and must deeply apologize. It is fortunate that you did not respond to his ramblings.

As you can tell, John has some problems but he has been a faithful employee. This does not in any way make acceptable his behavior. I must take a few days to digest this latest incident (he was also wearing my clothes during my absence) and decide on the proper course of action.

I am still very interested in your program. Tell me how we should proceed at this time. I will be home for at least six weeks.

Again, please ignore anything that John said. I'm afraid this time he went too far.

Best Wishes,

Gabe Kaplan

Date:	Fri, 28 Mar 2003 11:06:45 -0800
From:	"Brent" <brent@enrichyoulife.com>
Subject:	Re: Back home, must apologize
To:	gabe@gabekaplan.com

Gabe,

I just got back from out of town as well. I apologize for my delayed response.

I can offer you unlimited phone consultations for the duration of the three week mentoring period.

We'll create a customized plan to boost your success guaranteed.

thanks,
Brent

ROOTS

Date:	Thu, 13 Mar 2003 19:47:07 -0800 (PST)
From:	"Gabe Kaplan" <gabe@gabekaplan.com>
Subject:	Was I Adopted?
To:	bryan@orchidcell.com

Dear Bryan,

The Maryland lab suggested I get in touch with you. Let me start out by saying that in my opinion you guys got robbed on that OJ Simpson thing. What did you say the odds were that someone else killed those people, something like 80 to 1? That seems like an airtight case to me. I mean, how often do you see an 80-to-1 shot win at the track?

Not why I'm writing, though. I used to do a joke in my act where I wondered if I was adopted. "So one day I asked my father, 'I said, Ling Chow...was I adopted?' And he said (Chinese accent), 'No, you not adopted. You rented.'"

Little did people know the joke was based on a real concern. Ever since I was four my older sister would constantly tell me I was adopted. Now I had never heard the word "adopted" so I thought she was calling me an "apricot", which I kind of liked.

When I found out the difference I asked my parents about it and they assured me I was their natural child. But I thought their eye contact was minimal. Then I noticed I didn't look like them. My sister did. They were all blondes and sort of Nordic-looking. The seed of doubt had been planted and I could never quite shake it. Now that I'm a grown man I would like to put the matter to rest forever.

Would you be able to test my DNA and compare it to my sister's?

(Our parents have both passed.) Just tell me what kind of material you need me to send. As for my sister, she's not cooperating so we'll have to trick her to get her samples. If it turns out that I am adopted, can you use my DNA to find my real parents? Do you think they're alive? Would they ask me for things?

Best Wishes,

Gabe Kaplan
gabe@gabekaplan.com

PS If I send you pictures of my sister, my parents, and myself, could you give me an opinion based solely on the pictures?

Date:	Mon, 17 Mar 2003 07:14:52 -0600
From:	"Bryan" <bryan@orchidcell.com>
Subject:	Re: Was I Adopted?
To:	gabe@gabekaplan.com

Good day, Mr. Kaplan.

We at Orchid Cellmark would be happy to help you.
Upon discussion with several of our analysts as
well as a couple of our directors, it was decided
that nuclear DNA testing would be the preferred
method to help you find the answers you need.
However, to be successful using this method, you
would need to be certain that your sister is you
parents' natural child and not adopted. A blood
sample or oral swab from both of you is desireable
for testing, though a hair pulled from the root
may be used if absolutely necessary.

An alternative form of testing offered at Orchid
Cellmark is Mitochondrial DNA testing. This
form of testing would indicate whether or not
you and your sister are decendents of the same
maternal lineage. This testing would not provide
any information regarding paternity, thus it is
not as definitive as nuclear DNA testing. In your
case, Mitochondrial DNA testing can be performed
if one or both submitted samples are cut (or
broken) hairs that do not have a root attached
or if you suspect your sister may be adopted.

Please feel free to contact our Dallas, Texas
laboratory if you wish to proceed. You may get in
touch with our lead casework analyst, Ms. XXXX,
or our Forensics Manager, Ms. XXXXX, at 800-XXX-
XXXX for further information regarding sample
submission and testing costs.

Bryan
Forensic DNA Analyst
Orchid Cellmark Dallas

Date:	Sun, 23 Mar 2003 14:30:05 -0800 (PST)
From:	"Gabe Kaplan" <gabe@gabekaplan.com>
Subject:	Re: Was I Adopted: follow up.
To:	bryan@orchidcell.com

Dear Bryan,

Thank you very much for your informative reply. I have taken a while to mull things over. As much as I would like to know the answer, it seems that there is quite a bit involved in this testing. First of all, the tests themselves have long, intimidating names. Not to mention, I would have to get my sister's DNA without her suspecting anything. I don't know if you know my sister, but she's not prone to giving up things easily.

When you spoke to your analysts and directors, did you mention that I could get pictures of my sister, parents and myself and send them to you? The pictures I'm talking about are digital and have outstanding clarity and resolution. If everybody at the lab would be willing to take their best guess as to whether I could possibly be related to these people, that would be good enough for me. I could have some closure without spending a lot of money on Nuclear, Mitochondrial or whatchamacallit testing. I would be willing to pay you for your efforts and not hold you accountable if you made a mistake.

You could probably spot something in the pictures instantly, you're the Cellmark guys.

Best wishes,

Gabe Kaplan

PS I keep obsessing about what would happen if I tried to pull my sister's hair out at the root. Do you remember the sounds Jackie Gleason would make when he stubbed his toe?

Date:	Tue, 25 Mar 2003 06:52:42 -0600
From:	"Bryan" <bryan@orchidcell.com>
Subject:	Re: Was I Adopted: follow up.
To:	gabe@gabekaplan.com

Mr. Kaplan,

Since our business here at Orchid Cellmark
is forensic DNA testing, none of our
analysts are qualified or have been trained
to make the picture comparison to which
you refer. If anybody could do such a task
with any precision, which is doubtful in my
opinion, that would be a law enforcement
entity.

As for a sample obtained covertly from your
sister, a hair (or multiple hairs) taken
from her personal hair brush would work for
us provided you are highly confident that
no one else uses that hair brush. Another
item we have tested is a toothbrush, but
she would definitely notice such an article
missing from her vanity.

Feel free to forward any further questions
you may have. If you decide to use our
services, I will explain the procedure in
submitting any samples you have obtained.

Bryan
Forensic DNA Analyst
Orchid Cellmark Dallas

Date:	Wed, 26 Mar 2003 20:23:58 -0800 (PST)
From:	"Gabe Kaplan" <gabe@gabekaplan.com>
Subject:	Sister History Re: Adoption
To:	bryan@orchidcell.com

Dear Bryan,

You mentioned law enforcement. My sister hasn't always been a model citizen and has taken several vacations at taxpayers' expense. Her DNA is no stranger to FBI laboratories. That's why I thought you might know her. Her professional name is usually "Second-Story Sheila" or, for a while, "Cheyenne Sheila" back when she and her husband were rustling cattle out West. Do you have any idea how I would go about getting law enforcement to assist me in this project?

I once played golf with John Ashcroft. Would that mean anything? Or maybe I shouldn't even bring it up (I beat him).

Best Wishes,

Gabe Kaplan
gabe@gabekaplan.com

Date:	Thu, 27 Mar 2003 10:24:28 -0600
From:	"Bryan" <bryan@orchidcell.com>
Subject:	Re: Sister History Re: Adoption
To:	gabe@gabekaplan.com

Mr. Kaplan,

If you are looking for the most definitive results, DNA testing is your answer. Asking anyone to do a photograph comparison to determine relationship dates back to the 19th century and earlier. Would you have confidence in making such a comparison?

The FBI laboratory may be able to help you if they already have a DNA sample from your sister.

Federal Bureau of Investigation
935 Pennsylvania Avenue, NW
Washington, DC 20535
(202) 324-3000 (main number)

Bryan
Forensic DNA Analyst
Orchid Cellmark Dallas

Date:	Tue, 03 Jun 2003 11:51:54 -0700 (PDT)
From:	"Gabe Kaplan" <gabe@gabekaplan.com>
Subject:	Aren't You Judd Hirsch?
To:	ann.a.fox@eaxp.com

Dear Ms. Fox,

I was given your email address as the contact for Judd Hirsch. Although Judd and I have never met, an interesting situation developed around 1979 and continues to this day.

People still come up to me and say things like, "Aren't you the guy from Taxi, the serious guy, the only guy that didn't try to be funny? You're him, right?" I'm sure Judd must get asked all the time if he's Mr. Kotter.

Because of this ongoing confusion of the two of us, I took the liberty of calling a couple of the news magazine shows to see if we could capitalize on this. They said that they would love to have their cameras follow the both of us around for twenty-four hours. Here's the switch. Judd pretends he's me and I pretend I'm him. We would probably have to do this on a casual weekend. After all, I couldn't show up on the set of his latest project and say, "Hey, I'm here, I'm Judd Hirsch, I'm ready for my close up."

Nor could he show up at one of my supermarkets and claim he's me. But say he goes to the racetrack on Saturday and lets the word get out that he, Gabe Kaplan, thinks he's going to have a really hot day. Let's see how many of those race track people will know the difference. It could be great fun and the public loves stuff like this. It also shows that we both have a sense of humor and are both pretty good guys.

Let me know what Gabe, I mean Judd, thinks.

Gabe Kaplan
gabe@gabekaplan.com

PS If we both went to a Jewish retirement home, it could be hysterical.

Date:	Tue, 10 Jun 2003 14:49:14 -0700
From:	"Ann A. Fox" <ann.a.fox@eaxp.com>
Subject:	Re: Assuming A Pass?
To:	gabekaplan.com

Per your request, I have confirmed that Mr Hirsch schedule is such that he is not available at this time for your project and is sorry that he will have to pass.

I have just returned from vacation which caused a delay in my reply to you.

Ann Fox

Date:	Wed, 11 Jun 2003 20:31:52 -0700 (PDT)
From:	"Gabe Kaplan" <gabe@gabekaplan.com>
Subject:	Autographed Picture?
To:	ann.a.fox@eaxp.com

Ann,

Thanks for your help. When Judd gets a chance, could he send me an autographed picture saying, "Gabe, some people think we look alike. I don't know why, I'm much more attractive."

I'm trying to get funny vignettes from all the people I've been mistaken for. I've already got Billy Crystal, Franco Harris, and George Clooney.

Gabe
gabe@gabekaplan.com

*For Gabe . . . and for all those other things I did that you weren't blamed for.
With affection, Judd Hirsch*

Date:	Tue, 01 Jul 2003 21:09:14 -0700 (PDT)
From:	"Gabe Kaplan" <gabe@gabekaplan.com>
Subject:	Great Quip!
To:	ann.a.fox@eaxp.com

Ann,

Please thank Judd for sending me the picture. I'm glad he wrote his own quip, it was much better than the one I asked for.

Five more of the people I've been confused with have sent me pictures with quips. That makes the total nine, including Judd. I received a tenth, but there was no quip, just a signature, not even a "To Gabe". I won't say who it was, but he's a real "Meathead."

One time on Family Feud they surveyed 100 people and the question was "Men with Mustaches." There were five answers. Tom Selleck was number one, Hitler was second, and Burt Reynolds was fifth. Although I've never been mistaken for Hitler or Selleck, a couple of times people have thought I was Burt. So he's the next guy I'm writing to. I can't wait to see his quip.

I'm running out of actors I look like, so I'm thinking of getting into famous doctors, lawyers and politicians.

Thanks Again and Best Regards,

Gabe
gabe@gabekaplan.com

Date:	Wed, 18 Jun 2003 12:29:16 -0700 (PDT)
From:	"Gabe Kaplan" <gabe@gabekaplan.com>
Subject:	Arranging a Visit
To:	awc.pa@nellis.af.mil

Dear Nellis Air Force Base Public Affairs,

Over the last 20 years I have become an expert on UFOs, aliens, and space hovercrafts. My interest and involvement has been well documented by both the mainstream and fringe press. I even did some TV interviews about the subject, a result of me having been abducted on three different occasions. (I was only probed once.)

As a celebrity UFO expert/abductee I would like to nominate myself to be the first civilian to receive a government-sanctioned tour of Area 51. I know what's there already so I will not be surprised or shocked by anything I see.

After my visit I would divulge as much or as little information as you feel is appropriate. Just knowing that a celebrity UFO expert/abductee like myself has visited 51 would help people worldwide sleep more soundly. Also, I've heard whispers recently that there is an Area 52 which houses the latest aliens and their newest model spacecraft. I'm sure this is still "hush hush" and frankly I don't even know if 52 is close to 51. But, if possible, I'd like to be taken there, too. Again, you can count on my discretion.

In two months, on July 28th, I will be performing a special one-nighter in Las Vegas. I'll be working with The Captain and Tenille. The Captain is a believer, Tenille is not, but we're all good friends. This would be a perfect time for my long overdue visit. I will take your scheduling needs into account. The visit could be the day of, the day before, or the day after my performance.

My 12-year old daughter will be with me (a junior UFO buff), so let me know if you have a cafeteria or can provide her with a box lunch. If your chefs can cook up something like an Alien Burger she'd get a big kick out of that. She'd like to take some pictures with a few of the alien bodies and maybe dress up in a pathologist's uniform and pretend to perform an autopsy. Or something cute like that. This could be the first step toward mending fences. The Area 51 people and space freaks should be friends.

I want to go where no man has gone before,

Gabe Kaplan
gabe@gabekaplan.com

PS I can bring The Captain along on my tour but that's your call.

Date:	Thu, 26 Jun 2003 13:55:05 -0700
From:	"Maureen" <maureenpa@nellis.mil>
Subject:	FW: Nellis And Crepe Paper
To:	gabe@gabekaplan.com

Sir.

Please feel free to call me at the below number to discuss a tour.

Thanks for your interest in Nellis.

Mo
Maureen
AWFC Public Affairs

Date:	Thu, 26 Jun 2003 15:32:13 -0700 (PDT)
From:	"Gabe Kaplan" <gabe@gabekaplan.com>
Subject:	Excited About The Tour
To:	maureenpa@nellis.mil

Dear Maureen,

Thank you so much for your response. My daughter's competing at The Candyland Tournament in Anaheim this weekend. These tournaments have gotten so competitive, it's amazing. Last year two mothers got into a physical altercation. I had to be Mills Lane and break it up. What a bad message for the kids.

I'll be in touch on Monday and if a Nellis tour can be arranged that would be fantastic. In the interim, I'll try and send you the details of my request so you can be informed. That way you can let me know the possibilities when we speak.

Thanks again,

Gabe

Date:	Sun, 29 Jun 2003 23:31:52 -0700 (PDT)
From:	"Gabe Kaplan" <gabe@gabekaplan.com>
Subject:	My Original Request
To:	maureenpa@nellis.mil

Dear Maureen,

Well my daughter had her best year to date in the tournament. She got all the way to Queen Frostine and then was eliminated. Next year is her last year of eligibility, so let's keep our fingers crossed. Anyway, we'll hang around here for a couple of days, go to Disneyland, Knotts Berry Farm, and the Pancake House. Is my Area 51 tour approved?

Gabe

Date:	Mon, 30 Jun 2003 12:35:44 -0700
From:	"Maureen" <maureenpa@nellis.mil>
Subject:	Re: My Original Request
To:	gabe@gabekaplan.com
Cc:	a bunch of Air Force people

Mr Kaplan,

Thank you for your interest in Nellis AFB.
I think we have a misunderstanding. I'm not
familiar with Area 51 and have no idea how
you would get a tour of that which you are
describing. If you are interested in touring
Nellis Air Force Base and learning of our
advanced tactics, training and testing mission,
I would be happy to speak with you to see what
could be arranged. The tour would most likely
consist of a visit to the Air Force Thunderbirds
aerial demonstration team museum as well as our
threat training facility where we house captured
enemy aircraft and weapons.

Please call at your earliest convenience.

Mo
Maureen
AWFC Public Affairs

Date:	Mon, 07 Jul 2003 22:26:45 -0700 (PDT)
From:	"Gabe Kaplan" <gabe@gabekaplan.com>
Subject:	In Complete Agreement
To:	maureenpa@nellis.mil

Dear Maureen:

Hope you had a great 4th. My daughter and I did something unusual: We went swimming, had a cookout and watched fireworks.

I completely understand your last email. There is no Area 51 and there are no alien bodies or spaceships at Nellis or in any of the adjacent areas.

My July 28th visit is to see the Thunderbirds museum and the threat training facility. I will not discuss anything I see without the complete approval of Nellis Air Force Base.

Let me know if this email is satisfactory.

Best Regards,

Gabe Kaplan
gabe@gabekaplan.com

Date:	Wed, 09 Jul 2003 09:49:43 -0700
From:	"Maureen" <maureenpa@nellis.mil>
Subject:	Re: In Complete Agreement
To:	gabe@gabekaplan.com
Cc:	the same bunch of Air Force people

Sir.

If you can give me a call by the 15th of July we
may be able to work out a tour for you and your
daughter. I need to speak with you regarding
details.

Thanks,

Mo
Maureen
AWFC Public Affairs

Date: Wed, 23 Jul 2003 22:10:15 -0700 (PDT)
From: "Gabe Kaplan" <gabe@gabekaplan.com>
Subject: July 28th
To: maureenpa@nellis.mil

Dear Maureen,

It seems now that I will be flying in for my show on the 28th and leaving immediately afterwards.

Thank you for your offer to tour Nellis, but since we had something of a cat-and-mouse game going on, I wasn't sure if you were going to take me to Area 51 or not. I know it is the Air Force's position that you do military testing at Nellis, but Area 51 does not exist. How do they explain the thousands of people who have personal knowledge that it does? Did they just imagine what they saw? Maybe we're just a weird species who either wants to believe in strange phenomena or profit from other people's vulnerability to these beliefs.

Thanks again. I know you were just doing your job. Even though you were evasive, you tried to be as polite and accommodating as possible.

Regards,

Gabe
gabe@gabekaplan.com

PS I was rooting for Air Force when they lost to Notre Dame last year. I think Regis Philbin might be an alien.

THE UNHOLY ONE

Date:	Mon, 09 Dec 2002 11:26:13 -0800 (PST)
From:	"Gabe Kaplan" <gabe@gabekaplan.com>
Subject:	Body Piercing info
To:	brian@piercing.org

Dear Body Piercers:

One of the perks of being a celebrity is that I could always find younger women willing to bump bellies. Now at 52, that amount of interested jeune filles is steadily declining. Could it be that I just don't look hip anymore?

In your opinion, would body piercing help? I don't even have an earring so I'm a complete novice.

Which pierced body part do you find is the most attractive to young women?
Would one piercing be enough?
If any were in embarrassing spot could I count on your discretion?
How much does it hurt?
My religion forbids tattoos but doesn't say anything about holes. Does anyone ever get acupuncture and body piercing at the same time? My back's been bothering me.

Enough questions, please give me some information.

The unholy one,

Gabe Kaplan,
gabe@gabekaplan.com

Date:	Tue, 10 Dec 2002 17:38:59 -0500
From:	"Brian Skellie" <brian@piercing.org>
Subject:	Re: Body Piercing info
To:	gabe@gabekaplan.com
Cc:	gabe@gabekaplan.com

As far as attraction and piercing goes, it
certainly affords you the edge that you have
something exotic to explore. To undergo the
experience, a second of intense sensation rarely
described as pain is all that you would have to
endure. The challenge is mostly psychological and
spiritual. The anticipation and apprehension seem
the most trying aspects for most people who are
new to the experience, nikhedonia is my favorite
Hellenic expression for it. The healing process can
also be a great way to put you in touch with your
body.

You are assured a confidential and pleasant
experience. We have had the honor of being of
service to a handful of celebrities over the
last ten years in business, due to the reliable
standards of quality we have developed for
infection prevention and quick healing.

One of my closest friends is becoming a rabbi, and
he mentioned the mitzvah for piercing ears is well
established as a part of the Jubilee year. I pierced
his ears, nipples and the base of his penis on the
underside. He doesn't wear the ear jewelry but for
special occasions. As for the genitals, he obviously
doesn't show them off because of the Jewish value of
tzniut, modesty.

Of all of the possible places for a person to
pierce, probably the most entertaining for you
and your potential paramour would be the nipples.
They can be exposed somewhat under even modest

circumstances, and felt through clothing. They provide new levels of sensation and more fun to be had.

I am amused by your comment regarding acupuncture, as two of my colleagues are trained acupuncturists and doctors of Traditional Chinese Medicine. I am certain that they have included acupuncture in some ways in their procedures, though my job is primarily to prevent possible over stimulation of meridians by careful jewelry placement.

Glad to help, we'll be here to welcome you with a smile. We certainly do things differently here, and it's all based on making it easier for you.

The service is a flat fee of $50 for both, the jewelry, a small bar in titanium would be $33 and up per bar. A highly recommended option is to have both nipples pierced simultaneously with two of our staff, a tremendously positive and unique experience, only an extra $25.

You could make the jewelry change to nearly any color you like for free, if you please. We never use rings as initial jewelry, and encourage you consider them like high heeled shoes, kind of awkward and best used carefully or only for dress up.

Our procedure for nipple piercing

Please use the information on our http://www.piercing.org/pexy/technique/technique.html page for safety procedures for all piercing. As for the actual part where we make a hole and put in jewelry, that part is pretty simple.

1. We select custom fit jewelry

2. We have the client fill out a consent form

3. We explain and give printed recovery information

4. We sterilize the gloves, gauze, needle, and jewelry by a state of the art autoclave steam process

5. We bring the client to a private clean room used only for piercing services

6. We make the client feel comfortable, confident, and trustful

7. We put on a surgical mask and protective eyewear

8. We scrub our hands

9. We put on nitrile medical exam gloves

10. We mark the skin where the jewelry will live using a single use disposable surgical marker

11. We prepare the skin with a surgical cleanser

12. We put on sterilized gloves

13. We pick up the freshly sterilized gauze, drape, needle and jewelry

14. We put a sterile fabric drape with the window in the drape positioned over the area we are to decorate

15. We align the tissue by hand, like a surgeon would line up tissue to suture

16. We ask the client to take a deep breath and tell them that when they let it out, it is over

17. The client breathes out smoothly, and the skin is pricked gracefully, quickly and with great attention to aim

18. The jewelry, a barbell made of beautiful Titanium (surgical implant material), connects to the needle and gently follows it through

19. The ball is put into the hole in the bar and tightened

20. The client gets a first look and to live happily ever after with their new jewelry

In about 30 to 90 days, it should be finished healing, with no antiseptic, or soaking, or washing.
We encourage our clients to return for a checkup within the first 30 days to make sure everything is going well.
That would be it in a nutshell...

Brian Skellie
www.piercing.org

Acknowledgments

I WOULD LIKE TO THANK THE FOLLOWING PEOPLE: JOE BOLSTER, GABE ABELSON, AND JIM ALDEN FOR BEING GREAT SOUNDING BOARDS. MY AGENT, IAN KLEINERT, FOR BELIEVING IN THE PROJECT AND CONTINUALLY UTZING ME TO GET IT PUBLISHED. MY EDITOR, TRICIA BOCZKOWSKI, FOR REALIZING THAT FOUR-YEAR-OLD MATERIAL CAN STILL BE FUNNY. CARA BEDICK AND JANE ARCHER FOR THEIR VALUABLE ASSISTANCE. FINALLY ALL THE PEOPLE WHO REPLIED TO MY "SILLY NONSENSE" E-MAILS, WHETHER OR NOT THEY WERE INCLUDED IN THIS BOOK.